Harlequin®

Desire

"Harlequin Desires are better than
the best chocolate truffles in the world."
—*USA TODAY* Bestselling Author Leanne Banks

Look for all six
Special 30th Anniversary Collectors' Editions
from some of our most popular authors.

TEMPTED BY HER INNOCENT KISS
by Maya Banks
with "Never Too Late" by Brenda Jackson

BEHIND BOARDROOM DOORS
by Jennifer Lewis
with "The Royal Cousin's Revenge"
by Catherine Mann

THE PATERNITY PROPOSITION
by Merline Lovelace
with "The Sheik's Virgin" by Susan Mallery

A TOUCH OF PERSUASION
by Janice Maynard
with "A Lover's Touch" by Brenda Jackson

A FORBIDD
by Yvonn
with "For Love or Mon

CAUGHT IN T
by Jule
with "Billionaire's Baby" by

* * *

Find Harlequin Desire on Facebook,
www.facebook.com/HarlequinDesire,
or on Twitter, @desireeditors!

Dear Reader,

Harlequin Desire! What's not to love? Before I even considered writing a romance novel, I read tons of Desire novels. They captured my attention on so many levels. The authors were fantastic. Diana Palmer, Joan Hohl, Ann Major, Jennifer Greene. The stories drew me in with the power of passion and the exciting characters. I absolutely could not get enough of these books. I just sank into them with all my heart. They were better than any movie or TV show, and so much more satisfying. What could be better than watching a woman with some of my own insecurities tame a tough Desire hero?

Speaking of what's not to love, how about those Desire men? Pure alpha, sexy and always wealthy. It's so nice not to have to worry about money, isn't it? For our Desire heroines (or us, the reader), the Desire man is definitely forbidden. He's got trouble written all over him in bold capital letters. But somehow we can't resist him. Somehow, underneath it all, we know he has a heart that needs to be healed and we are the ones who can do it.

What I love about the stories is the *gasp* factor. I love it when a book takes an unexpected turn. I love to be shocked a little. Don't you? So here's to your next thirty years, Harlequin Desire. Keep bringing us men who make our hearts pound and women who make them fall in love....

Wishing you your heart's most passionate Desire...

xo,

Leanne Banks

JULES BENNETT

CAUGHT IN THE SPOTLIGHT

ISBN-13: 978-0-373-73161-9

CAUGHT IN THE SPOTLIGHT

Copyright © 2012 by Harlequin Books S.A.

The publisher acknowledges the copyright holders of the individual works as follows:

CAUGHT IN THE SPOTLIGHT
Copyright © 2012 by Jules Bennett

BILLIONAIRE'S BABY
Copyright © 2003 by Harlequin Books S.A.
Leanne Banks is acknowledged as the author of this work.

Recycling programs for this product may not exist in your area.

www.Harlequin.com

Printed in U.S.A.

CONTENTS

Books by Jules Bennett

Harlequin Desire

Her Innocence, His Conquest #2081
Caught in the Spotlight #2148

Silhouette Desire

Seducing the Enemy's Daughter #2004
For Business...or Marriage? #2010
From Boardroom to Wedding Bed? #2046

Other titles by this author available in ebook format.

JULES BENNETT

Jules's love of storytelling started when she would get in trouble as a child and would tell her parents her imaginary friend Mimi did it. Since then, her vivid imagination has taken her down a path she'd only dreamed of.

When Jules isn't spending time with her wonderful supportive husband and two daughters, you will find her reading her favorite authors. Though she calls that time "research." She loves to hear from readers! Contact her at authorjules@gmail.com, visit her website at www.julesbennett.com or send her a letter at P.O. Box 396, Minford, OH 45653. You can also visit her fan page on Facebook or follow her on Twitter (@JulesBennett).

Dear Reader,

Glamorous lifestyles, lies and betrayal...welcome to Hollywood.

I've always had a fascination with old movies and the icons who starred in them. Audrey Hepburn, Vivien Leigh and Elizabeth Taylor are just a few on my list of faves for their flawless beauty and classy style.

I knew I wanted to bring my love of old Hollywood into my Desire stories. And what better way to launch my new Hollywood family than with the 30th anniversary celebration of Harlequin Desire! Alpha men who exude power and the women who challenge them? What's not to love?

Combining the sexiness of Hollywood with the complex, emotional plots Desire is known for was a dream! I'm so thrilled to introduce the Dane family. Bronson Dane is a hotshot producer who exudes power and passion, but he has no clue the secret that's about to be revealed when his mother's new personal assistant, Mia Spinelli, comes onto the scene.

I hope you'll fall in love with this family as I have, and stay tuned as I uncover more lies and betrayal in the two follow-up books with the other Dane siblings. I'd love to hear what you think of my Hollywood family. Drop me a line via my website, www.julesbennett.com.

Happy reading!

Jules

To the ladies who are always there
to talk me out of my panicky state: Leanne Banks,
Lynne Marshall, Janice Maynard and Charlene Sands. I'm
blessed to call you not only critique partners, but friends.

And to my fabulous editor, Shana Smith,
for loving my idea of doing a series set around the glitz,
glamour and gossip of Hollywood.

CAUGHT IN
THE SPOTLIGHT

Jules Bennett

One

When a dripping-wet female yelled his name, Bronson Dane didn't even try to stop his eyes from roaming over all of her.

With only a short white towel covering her glistening dark, Italian skin, his mother's personal assistant of only six months certainly knew how to catch a man's attention.

"Mr. Dane," she repeated, clutching the towel to her chest with both hands. She'd stopped short as she'd stepped from the bath when she saw him standing at the desk in his mother's adjoining office.

"Formalities are unnecessary when you're only wearing water droplets and a towel. Call me Bronson." He shoved his hands in his pants pockets, thankful he'd shed his jacket because, damn, the temperature just rose at least ten degrees. "Where is my mother and why are you showering in her private bath?"

Wide eyes, nearly as dark as her ebony hair, blinked in

rapid succession. "Olivia is gone for the day. I often use the gym, and since I'm working this afternoon, she told me just to freshen up here instead of running back to my guest cottage."

Bronson muttered a curse at his naive mother. It was bad enough Mia Spinelli lived on the Dane estate, but now she was given free rein of the house? Hadn't his mother learned her lesson from the last "loyal" assistant? When would the woman realize she couldn't trust everyone who looked innocent?

This was Hollywood, for pity's sake. Lies and manipulation were as common as breast implants and collagen injections.

"I'm sorry, Mr. Dane. I had no idea anyone would be coming by," Mia continued, squaring her shoulders as if having a conversation wearing only a scrap of terry cloth was normal. "Weren't you supposed to be shooting in Australia until next week?"

"Call me Bronson," he reminded her, gritting his teeth at the floral aroma wafting from the bathroom. "The movie wrapped a week early. I stopped by to talk to my mother about the film festival next week. Did she say when she'd be back?"

"She'll be back later in the afternoon. She's having lunch with her attorney to go over the final contract for her next book." The knuckles on the hand fisting her towel between her breasts turned white as she crossed the room. "If you'll excuse me, I dropped my toiletry bag on the desk chair when I came in because the phone was ringing."

Before she could pass by him, he blocked her and reached for the simple black bag from the leather desk chair. She grabbed for it, but he held the small bag out to the side, away from her grasp.

He didn't trust her, especially since she'd just come off

the heels of working for the one man he despised in the industry, Anthony Price. He loathed the man with every fiber of his being. But he certainly didn't want to think about all those reasons now.

His mother had assured him that Mia was "a doll" and completely trustworthy and dependable. His sister, Victoria, had jumped on the Mia bandwagon as well, stating that Mia was such a joy and pleasure to be around. When they'd chatted on the phone last, Victoria had gone so far as to say that she'd instantly clicked with their mother's new assistant.

Granted, Mia had been around for six months, but was that enough time for his mother and sister to be such diehard Mia Spinelli fans?

Bronson wasn't blind, though. Anthony sending his assistant here to snoop was really sinking to a low he never expected.

The rumors of Mia and Anthony's relationship were anything but businesslike. And that irked him even more. The fact his mother had hired Mia while he'd been on location in Australia still grated on him. True, his mother could have any assistant she chose, but why bring in one fresh from his nemesis?

The Hollywood rumor mill had pegged the mesmerizing Mia as the main problem in Anthony's rocky marriage. Whom Mia slept with was none of his concern, but it *was* his business if she was taking Dane family secrets back to her lover.

Bronson and his mother were secretly working on a huge film that he knew the media would die to get their hands on. He and his mother had worked for years honing this project, and he had no doubt Anthony Price, Hollywood's top director, wanted to know just what the big secret was.

Just because his mother wasn't suspicious didn't mean he'd be letting his guard down any time soon.

Bronson intended to find out just what this conveniently placed assistant's intentions were before she uncovered the script and slid back in between Anthony's sheets with it in hand. The thought of this sexy siren in bed with the devil made his stomach knot up.

He thrust the bag her way because he needed her to get dressed. Whether he trusted her or not had no bearing on matters; she was fresh from the shower smelling of something sexy and floral—her own because that certainly wasn't his mother's scent—and he was having a hard time focusing on the task at hand.

Not to mention that he was not one bit happy with the immediate physical attraction he felt to his enemy's lover.

"Get dressed. We'll talk."

With a slight nod, she turned, crossed the room and entered the still-steamy bath, shutting the door at her back. He had no room on his plate for lustful feelings, and he was a damn fool for even letting them creep into his thoughts. His main concern right now was to keep his mother and his fashion designer sister out of any more scandal.

His mother's last assistant had stolen nearly half a million dollars from Olivia's personal account over the span of several months. The media loved feeding off the Dane name right now, which is why they needed to be a bit more cautious about whom they let into their lives—especially if he had any hopes of keeping this script under wraps.

Was it any wonder his blood pressure had soared since he stepped into his mother's office? Olivia Dane was an icon, and the media would love to get some dirt on her—though he doubted there was any. They had a way of twisting even the innocent to make them look sordid.

Olivia Dane had been Hollywood's sweetheart, had

starred in more films than any other female in the industry and had been dubbed the "Grand Dane" years ago. The media loved her. Which is precisely why he needed to keep a close watch on her new assistant.

The bathroom door opened once again and Mia emerged wearing crisp white capris and a black, sleeveless button-down shirt. She had twisted her long dark hair into some sort of knot at the nape of her neck. Her feet were still bare, except for the subtle pink polish on her toes. A simple gold locket lay in the open V of her shirt.

Everything about this woman screamed innocence and simplicity, so how the hell did she end up working for the most glamorous woman in Hollywood?

Olivia had told him how impeccable Mia's credentials were and Mia's reasons for leaving her job with Anthony. Supposedly she didn't want to be the cause of any more rumors and aid in destroying Anthony's marriage.

His mother had said she admired a woman who put others' needs ahead of her own. She assured him the background check also confirmed her initial thoughts—Mia was flawless and perfect for the job.

A background check could easily make a person look good on paper, and Mia had certainly appeared to be innocent as an angel, but Bronson wanted to get to know more about the quiet, subtle Miss Spinelli. The one who, no matter what line she fed his mother, still may be sleeping with—and possibly spying for—his enemy.

And fate had just handed him the perfect opportunity. What better way to get to know someone than a little one-on-one time? With the exotic, sexy ambiance of the Cannes Film Festival next week, how could she resist succumbing to his charms as his escort? He hadn't been dubbed *People's* Sexiest Man Alive for nothing.

"I have a proposition for you," he told her. "You're traveling to Cannes with my mother. Correct?"

Mia nodded.

"There are ceremonies every evening with parties afterward. I want you to escort me to those events."

"Escort you?" she asked, eyes wide. "But I'm only going to work with Olivia, and I hadn't planned on attending any of the evenings' festivities."

He hadn't planned on asking her to be his escort, but he also hadn't planned on his first impression of her covered in iridescent droplets and wearing nothing but a piece of terry cloth. God knows he could invite any woman he knew, but he really didn't want to have to entertain and make sure some diva was properly pampered. This woman, this virtual stranger, would be the ideal companion. He'd been on location nearly the entire time she'd been employed by his mother. He couldn't think of a better venue to get to know Mia than to have her as his "date" for five nights in a row.

"I don't think this is a good idea," Mia said, taking a seat behind his mother's desk and booting up the computer. "I'm pretty busy with Olivia, and I know we'll be working just as hard in Cannes because she's trying to finish this book by midsummer."

Bronson stood on the other side of the desk, watching Mia's delicate, ringless fingers fly over the keyboard. "I assure you, my mother will have no problem with your being my escort. You just worry about getting to the plane on time and packing light. I'll have Victoria ship all the dresses you'll need. She's a whiz in a pinch."

She looked up from the screen, licking her naked lips. "But why me?"

"Why not you?" he countered, liking this idea more and more.

"I'm just an assistant."

Bronson shrugged. "All the more reason. Unless you don't want to be seen with me because of your recent scandal with your previous employer." He leaned in close and whispered, "Or you have a jealous lover."

Mia's eyes widened. "I can't believe that out of all the women you know, you'd want to take me."

Her swift dodge of his question wasn't very subtle, but he'd let it pass. For now.

"I won't lie." Leaning on his palms on the edge of the mahogany desk, Bronson offered a crooked grin and eased back just a bit so he didn't seem too overbearing. "I'm protective of my mother. I'm using this as a prime opportunity to get to know you better."

A sinful, beautiful smile spread across her face. "I understand being protective about family. In that case, I'd love to attend with you, as long as Olivia doesn't mind."

Bronson stood straight up and returned her smile. "She won't. Trust me."

Trust me.

It had been four days since Bronson had flashed his sexy smile and charmed her into turning her working trip into something more social.

And she should've flat-out told him no. He wouldn't have asked her to attend parties and ceremonies with him, and he sure as hell wouldn't have asked her to trust him, if he knew the secret she held. A secret that would ruin his family's tight bond.

Mia shook the guilt off and concentrated on her immediate mission: she was in Cannes and she was going to be waltzing into glamorous events on the arm of Hollywood's sexiest bachelor. She had to look better than her best.

Which shouldn't be a problem. Looking back at her

were five—yes, five—glamorous Victoria Dane original designs. Mia took a step back in her luxurious suite, unable to catch her breath. Olivia had told her that Victoria always kept multiple designs on hand for any star who needed a dress last minute.

Cinderella and her fairy godmother had nothing on Mia and this amazing array of glitzy dresses.

She had to keep reminding herself that she was just an assistant, but Mia certainly felt like a star as she spun in a little-girl-like circle, giddiness overwhelming her.

Was this really happening? Was she really in Cannes working for Olivia Dane by day, dressing up in a Victoria Dane gown at night and mingling with celebrities on the arm of hotshot producer Bronson Dane? Did she hit the job jackpot or what?

She and Olivia had worked a couple hours on the long flight over and Olivia had given Mia the rest of the day off. Of course, Mia figured Olivia was shopping at all the specialty shops.

Mia smiled as she recalled how surprised, yet excited Olivia was when she'd learned Mia was escorting Bronson to the parties and awards ceremonies. The Grand Dane had smiled, clasped her jeweled fingers together and said, "Wonderful."

Everything about working for the Grand Dane was incredible. Mia had been scared to leave Anthony at first, but now she knew this was the best decision for everyone. She'd come to love him like family—though not in the way the family-wrecking tabloids had portrayed their relationship. She hoped he could put his marriage back together.

Mia's heart ached for Anthony. Never once had their relationship turned intimate, but the tabloids assumed and printed the worst, in turn hurting his wife. Yes, they'd spent a lot of time together, but they were always working.

Mia knew Olivia believed her, but what about Bronson? Did he also assume the worst about her? More than likely. There was no love lost between the two Hollywood big shots, which meant he probably believed the rumors. He'd already implied as much.

Hopefully, her actions would win his trust in time. He'd had his fair share of scandal in the media. Surely he didn't believe everything he heard or read. Hollywood certainly wasn't known for honesty.

And she'd never expected anything like this when she'd come to work for Olivia. When she'd been employed by Anthony, she'd traveled with him to film sites, but never, ever to a glamorous film festival. And here she was in Cannes. Just the trip itself was thrilling, but adding all the extras on top of that was fabulous.

First, she'd expected a simple room, not a suite, and she never, in her wildest dreams, thought she'd be treated like a princess when she was just…an assistant. But she'd take this once-in-a-lifetime opportunity and not question the whys.

With a delicate touch, because God knew she'd never be able to cover the expense of just one of these dresses, even though her pay was very generous, she looked over the gowns as she envisioned dancing the night away in each one.

Spending money on clothes was not a priority in Mia's life, unlike many women who lived in Hollywood. But she certainly wouldn't turn down the opportunity to wear these classy, elegant designs.

Would she be dancing with Bronson all night? Would her body press against his as they swayed? She'd be lying to herself if she pretended she hadn't thought of being close to him, feeling his arms around her.

More than likely he had a whole slew of women who

danced with him at such events, but he'd chosen her to escort him. What did that mean? And he'd gone to the trouble of getting his sister involved. Did he just want to get to know her better, as he'd said? She could understand that, but somewhere deep inside she thought he must find her attractive or he wouldn't have asked her to accompany him every single night.

The memory of his eyes taking in her bare skin when he'd caught her coming out of the shower had her body humming. She wasn't vain, but she also wasn't stupid. Bronson hadn't been immune to the fact she'd been pretty much naked.

Reality check.

To think that Bronson Dane found her attractive sounded absurd, even in her own head. He worked with movie starlets, dated models and had literally seen women who exemplified perfection in the flesh. He'd even been engaged to a stunning makeup artist. But still, his eyes had widened on seeing her, and the muscle had ticked in his jaw. Her body heated again when she recalled how close they'd been as he'd held her bag away from her. He'd smelled so…masculine, powerful. Sexy.

Mia pulled the short, black, chiffon dress from the closet and held it in front of her as she turned to the full-length mirror. This would be for the first party. All the dresses were gorgeous, but this one—this would make the biggest impact. She wanted Bronson's first impression of her in Cannes to be memorable.

The simplicity of the black gown and her black hair would complement each other and hopefully help her blend in with the rich and famous. She certainly didn't want to be an embarrassment on Bronson's arm. She may have immature thoughts, but she wanted him to notice her as more than his mother's assistant.

Nerves danced around in her belly. How could she even compare to the arm candy Bronson normally had draped over him?

A laugh escaped her as she hung the dress back up. Had she just compared herself to arm candy? She wasn't here to try to win Bronson over as her boyfriend or even her lover…but that didn't stop her from wishing to be noticed by Hollywood's sexiest bachelor. What woman wouldn't want to be desired by such a strong, powerful man who ranked his loving family at the top of his priority list? There wasn't a woman alive who wouldn't want to be part of his inner circle.

But amid the excitement and arousal, guilt gnawed away at Mia as she pulled another dress from the closet. How could she take so much from this family when she knew a secret that could very well destroy their perfect happiness?

Unfortunately, the secret wasn't hers to reveal. And since she had come to care about all the key players, she felt torn between her loyalty to her former employer and her loyalty to her current employer.

Right now all she could do was keep her own counsel and enjoy herself in one of the most exotic, memorable places on earth. Borrowing trouble that was utterly out of her hands wouldn't help ease the guilt or make the nearly forty-year-old secret disappear.

Mia's cell rang, breaking into her thoughts. She pulled her phone from her pocket and hit the Talk button.

"Hello?"

"I trust you found the dresses to your satisfaction."

Mia's gaze traveled back to the open closet. "Yes, Bronson, they're gorgeous. I could never thank you or Victoria enough."

"And the jewelry is all to your liking?" he asked. "If not, I can call the jeweler and have some pieces traded out."

Mia's eyes went to the dresser where velvet boxes were stacked. She hadn't even opened them, but she knew the contents were surely more glamorous than anything she'd ever seen.

She fingered the simple locket around her neck. "Everything is more than I'd hoped for. Thank you."

"Tonight's viewing begins at seven-thirty," he went on. "We have to be on the red carpet by quarter to seven, so I'll meet you down in the lobby by the elevator at six-thirty."

Without another word, he hung up. Mia didn't quite know what to make of his abruptness. On the jet en route to Cannes he'd made idle chitchat—nothing personal. At times she'd feel someone staring at her and turn to see those crystal-blue eyes on her as if he were just as intrigued with her as she was with him—at least, she liked to think that was the reason. And when she caught him, he didn't even pretend that he hadn't been studying her. But why would a strong, powerful playboy be shy or coy? He could have any woman he wanted, and that woman would gladly follow those endless baby blues anywhere. She was no exception.

She was finding, in the few encounters she'd had with Bronson, that he was a hard man to get to know, especially when he delivered a twenty-second phone call that was straight and to the point and hung up before she could even ask a question.

Mia sighed as she padded to the bath. A nice, long bubble bath would do her nerves some good. With Olivia out shopping with some friends for the day, Mia could just relax.

Or as much as she could relax with a damning secret preying on her mind. She'd had nothing but high hopes when she'd accepted this job as assistant to the Grand Dane of Hollywood. But then she'd accepted the position nearly a week before learning Olivia's best-kept secret. If only she'd left Anthony sooner and not worked during her two weeks' notice, she wouldn't have this guilt weighing on her.

So many times over the last six months she wished she didn't know the secret. Then maybe her job wouldn't be so difficult. But she did know. And eventually the truth would come out and damage Hollywood's most beloved family. The Danes.

All this secrecy bubbling inside her forced her mind back to another time, another secret that had hurt those she loved.

Her mother had once asked her to keep a secret, but at the tender age of five, Mia didn't think that meant to keep it from her father. Ultimately, the truth tore her family apart, taking the lives of her parents and sending Mia into a long line of foster homes. And even after twenty-five years, the guilt and heartache that followed her, haunted her, was just as strong and powerful as ever.

She knew she needed to keep this secret. No way would she cause another disaster. And this explosion she could see coming. She would keep this secret out of loyalty to a friend and respect to the key players.

After pouring an enormous amount of jasmine-scented bubblebath into the running water, Mia stepped into the round, sunken tub with a one-way window overlooking a lavish garden. She settled down into the skin-tingling hot water and sighed as she looked out the glass.

What would Bronson think once he saw her tonight? Would he be disappointed? Would he be attracted? Anthony had reminded her about Bronson's playboy style. He'd warned her not to get involved or, worse, attached to a man who was known for the revolving door in his bedroom.

Even though she'd worked for Anthony for three years,

she'd never once seen Anthony and Bronson in the same room. She'd certainly seen the tabloids showcasing the bitterness between the two Hollywood powerhouses, but anytime she questioned Anthony about it, he'd laugh it off. He was always joking, always carefree. The very opposite of Bronson.

But the tabloids' speculation about their alleged affair was no laughing matter. Neither she nor Anthony found the assumptions amusing. She'd seen firsthand the destruction a photo and boldface caption could cause.

She was eternally grateful that Olivia had given her a chance, and believed in her ability to do her job, and not focused on what the rumor mill portrayed her as—a liar.

And now she was in Cannes getting ready for one of the largest film festivals in the world.

With excitement and curiosity spiraling through her, Mia slid a handful of hot bubbles up over her shoulders. She only hoped the two men didn't get into another verbal altercation. The press was always so greedy when it came to pictures of the two most powerful men in movies having a public disagreement.

There had to be a way to bridge the hatred between Bronson and Anthony, and with her current position she could be that link. Because once Bronson learned that Anthony was the child Olivia had given up for adoption nearly forty years ago, he'd have even more hatred for the man than he did now.

She hadn't been able to save her own family, but maybe, just maybe, she could bring this family together.

TWO

Bronson's breath caught. He knew his mouth had dropped open, but nothing could pull his gaze from the sight coming toward him.

He hadn't thought it possible, but as Mia walked toward him in a Victoria Dane original, she looked even sexier than she had in just a towel.

Mia wore his sister's design as if she'd been made to model the one-of-a-kind dress on a runway in Milan or Paris. Or as if she'd been made to torture unsuspecting men like him.

He'd been feeling guilty about not picking her up at her suite, and now he knew that was a wise decision because there were very few steps from the door to the bed.

"I have to say, it's not often I'm speechless." Bronson lifted Mia's slender hand to his lips. "I'm glad you're going in on my arm."

Mia offered a sexy, confident smile. "Well, that makes two of us."

If this were any woman other than his mother's assistant, an assistant he still had serious doubts about, Bronson could've talked her out of that thin, flowy dress in a matter of seconds. And, who knows, he still could get her out of that dress. They were here for nearly a week, and this was only the first night. After all, he did need to spend some one-on-one time with her, didn't he?

Damn if she wouldn't be turning some heads tonight. Jealousy stabbed him in the chest. What did he care that men looked? So long as they didn't touch. For now, she was his. Anthony's loss made this seduction all the more enjoyable.

"Shall we?" he asked, slipping her arm through his.

She fit against him as they walked through the open lobby toward the glow of the sunset streaming in the etched-glass doors. Her heels clicked against the marble floor, the jasmine scent he'd associated with her wafting around him. Everything about her mocked him. He wanted her, but he didn't trust her. His emotions were all jumbled because of this intriguing woman, and he didn't like this lack of control. That in itself should make him dislike her, but she oozed sex appeal and confidence, and Bronson knew he would have her before the week's end.

When they reached the door, he placed a hand on the small of her back to escort her out…and encountered bare skin. If he thought she was sexy from the front with that low cowl-neck design that enhanced her perfect breasts, she was sinful from the back with the chiffon draping as low as legally possible without being indecent.

A sexy back got him every time. Of course, he was beginning to think every physical attribute of this Italian beauty got to him. Great. Just what he needed, an out-of-control libido to hinder his judgment about this woman…as if he weren't having enough issues with that. The fact she may have slept with his enemy should have been enough to turn him off. But damn if he wasn't stubborn and all the more defiant when he saw something, or someone, he wanted.

He had to hand it to his sister. When she'd picked the dress, she'd nailed the style that accentuated Mia's height, curves and sensual features. That's why Victoria was so sought after by every star in America—and why men were sent reeling by the women who wore the designs.

"Victoria sure knows how to make a woman feel pretty," Mia told him, seeming to read his mind as they walked beneath a canopy of lush palms and thick foliage beside the water's edge that led toward the red carpet. "I have to admit, I tried on every single one of those dresses. They're all my favorite."

Bronson hadn't removed his hand from her back and he didn't intend to. She was too soft, too feminine, too…everything.

The perfect spy for Anthony.

"Victoria knows how to make beautiful women look even more breathtaking."

Mia's gaze shot to his. "Thank you."

He stepped in front of her just before they reached the area with the camera flashes of the paparazzi and the red carpet. "I should be thanking you," he told her, then bent to whisper in her ear, "Because of you, I'll be the envy of every man here tonight."

A soft, visible shudder produced a shaky smile. "I doubt that, but thank you again."

She was serious. Most women in Hollywood loved showing off their bodies…God knows they'd paid enough for their enhancements. But as he studied Mia's dark, sultry eyes, he realized she was the minority. She may have trembled at his words, but she didn't believe him.

That was just fine, since he was still leery of her, as well. But he would uncover the true Mia soon enough. And if uncovering her from that wispy black dress was involved, well, that wouldn't be a hardship.

Anything to stick close to the alluring Mia Spinelli.

Flashes of lights, clicks of cameras and shouts of Bronson's name from every direction followed them as they made their way up the red carpet toward the steps leading into the Marché du Film Theater.

Mia couldn't believe this. Simply couldn't believe she was in Cannes, wearing a Victoria Dane design on the red carpet with Bronson's strong hand on her bare back. She took mental images of every moment because she knew, once she got back to the real world of "assisting," this would all be a wonderful, distant memory.

Though, she had a feeling the tingling from Bronson's touch would linger long after tonight. And that was just fine with her. Mercy, the man was potent.

She allowed him to lead her from camera to camera, giving a subtle nudge to her back when he wanted to move on to the next one. Did celebrities ever tire of this attention? Did they enjoy being photographed at every twist and turn? Probably not, but this was all so new to her, she was loving every minute.

But she'd worked in the industry, albeit in the background, long enough to know the camera caught everything. Would viewers see the Cinderella-like euphoria she drifted in? Would it capture the smile on her face that said she was having the time of her life, even though she hadn't been to a viewing, ceremony or post-party yet? She certainly hoped the sometimes unforgiving lens didn't zero in on her nerves and shaky hands.

"They're wondering why you're here on my arm," Bronson whispered in her ear as they turned to another camera. "Relax."

"Easy for you to say," she whispered.

His thumb stroked her back. "I've seen you wearing a scrap of terry cloth and water droplets, surely you can relax for a few cameras."

Did he have to keep bringing up that mortifying experience? Or perhaps he brought it up because he wasn't totally unaffected by her....

"You aren't the one who's been accused of having an affair with your boss." A horrifying experience.

He laughed, flashing his signature charming smile, no doubt giving the greedy paparazzi the snapshot they'd been after. "That's what makes you even more intriguing. They don't know what to expect."

They moved down the red carpet as more celebrities arrived, pleasing the rest of the media that awaited. Mia couldn't believe all the stars standing so close to her looking glamorous and flawless. Everyone smiled, waving to various cameras and gave brief interviews to the press.

True, she didn't like the limelight, but the recent rumors had given her no choice. The media ate up any type of scandal. And while Mia wasn't thrilled with having her life in the news, she would sacrifice her privacy if it meant taking the heat off Anthony long enough for him to rebuild his marriage. The media would no doubt speculate about her being a bed hopper, but she knew the truth.

"Let them speculate," she murmured. "I have nothing to be ashamed of."

"Let's head on inside," he told her and waved as a camera flashed in their faces. "I'm sure my mother is already wondering why we're not in our seats. She's always an hour early for these things so she can mingle."

Mia held on to Bronson's arm as she started up the red-carpeted steps. "And you don't like to mingle?"

He shrugged. "I mingle plenty at the after parties."

Mia laughed. "You're a man of few words. Aren't you?"

"When it's time to talk, I talk. Time to work, I work." He looked down at her, steely blue eyes darting to her lips. "Time to play, I definitely play."

A shiver rippled up her spine, stemming straight from that powerful stare. Fantastic. Just one heavy-lidded bedroom gaze and she had zings shooting through her body into every nook and cranny, making her even more attracted to the playboy on her arm.

"Any more questions?" he whispered in her ear, so close his warm breath tickled her cheek.

He may be quiet, but perhaps that's why he had a reputation as the master seducer. The subtle brush of his fingertips across her bare back, the whispers and those ocean-blue eyes—the man was charming seduction in stealth mode.

She turned, their mouths nearly touching. "I'll take a rain check."

Bronson leaned back just a hair and laughed. "And I'm sure you'll redeem it soon."

She smiled as they entered the grand foyer. "Count on it."

"Vous êtes trop genre."

Bronson jerked his head around at the flawless French that came from Mia's glossy lips as she spoke to a popular French producer. She laughed, patted the elderly man's beefy arm and turned back to Bronson.

"Sorry about that," Mia told him, beautiful smile still in

place. "On my way back from the chocolate fountain Mr. du Muir stopped me and we started chatting."

Chatting? In French? First she shows up in the lobby looking like sin in stilettos, teasing him with upswept hair and a bare back that just begged his hands to explore more, and then she conducts a conversation in French that sounded as if she'd been living in France her whole life.

"I forgot you were fluent in French," he told her, taking a champagne flute as a waiter walked by. He handed her the glass and an embossed napkin. "Mother told me you have an ear for languages." Not to mention he'd seen it on her background reports.

"I speak French, Spanish and Italian." She took a sip of champagne, leaving her plump pink lips moist, inviting.

"You even had the sexy accent down. You sure you're not an actress?" He only half joked.

Not once at the Marché du Film opening night film earlier or since they'd entered the Icon Picture party had she acted shy or uncomfortable. She'd lit up the red carpet with her smile and sultry gaze into the cameras, and Bronson knew without a doubt that when he saw their pictures in a tabloid, his eyes would be glued to this Italian beauty. There wasn't a man drawing breath who would blame him for being infatuated with her.

How many times over the past few years had she escorted Anthony Price to events? He'd never seen her, but then he hadn't been looking and didn't care who Anthony entertained. At least not at that point.

"Not an actress," she assured him with a smile. "I just find speaking another language romantic and mysterious."

"Romantic and mysterious?" Bronson leaned in so only she could hear. "The perfect description of my date tonight, wouldn't you say? Makes me want to uncover more of you."

Bronson leaned back, eager to see her eyes, even more

eager to hear her response. But Mia's dark gaze darted over his shoulder. Bronson turned to see what she was looking at, and the moment was gone.

"Oh, there's your mother." Mia waved, standing on her tiptoes.

"Darling!" Olivia closed the gap and kissed Mia's cheek. "So sorry I've been scarce since the showing. I've been catching up with old friends. There's quite a buzz about the beauty on my son's arm. There's not a man who can keep his eyes off you, my dear."

Mia laughed. "Oh, please. Every woman here is stunning."

Not like you. God, the words nearly came out of his mouth. But it was true. There wasn't a woman in Cannes right this minute who compared to Mia.

Focus. He wasn't here to get played by this woman—he was here to see what the hell she truly wanted from his family. There wasn't a doubt in his mind that Anthony had some kind of agenda behind Mia's career move. But he didn't have to worry about his mother saying anything to her personal assistant about the script they'd been working on. It was just as important to her that nothing be revealed until they were both ready.

And, if Mia turned out to be as clean and innocent as her background check indicated, then he would let her be. But if he found out she was indeed working for Anthony, they both would rue the day they decided to cross the Danes.

Bronson kissed his mother's cheek. "It's a shame Victoria couldn't join us this year."

Olivia smiled. "Working hard on a big celebrity wedding trumps us, darling. That girl does work herself to death."

Bronson laughed. "Says the pot about the kettle."

Olivia wrapped an arm around Bronson's waist in a half hug. "I'm proud of all my children for their hard work."

Bronson was about to say something else, but his thought was lost as he looked to Mia. A flash of pain darted through her eyes.

"You're all very lucky to have each other." Mia took a sip of champagne. "Does Victoria usually attend, as well?"

"Almost always," Olivia said. "She designed many of the dresses you see here tonight, and she loves nothing more than to admire her work up close."

Bronson didn't know about the other clients, but he was sure as hell happy with the dress she'd chosen for Mia. And he couldn't help but wonder what other taunting designs would adorn Mia during their trip. What dress he would ultimately unwrap her from.

God help him. This was only night one.

"It's getting late." Olivia lifted her face, placing a kiss on Bronson's cheek. "See you tomorrow. Mia, I'll see you first thing in the morning."

Mia smiled and nodded. "I'll be at your suite by eight."

As his mother disappeared beneath sparkling chandeliers into the sea of glitz, glamour and overflowing champagne fountains, Bronson turned back to Mia, who was placing her empty flute on the tray of a passing waiter.

Mia smothered a yawn. "I'm still a bit jet-lagged."

He hated that the evening was drawing to a close, but it was late and he had an early meeting. "Then I'll escort you to your room."

With a warm smile that threatened to lure him in, Mia placed a slender hand on his arm. "No need to leave because I am, Bronson. I'm sure you have many more associates who'd love to chat with you."

He shrugged. "It's well after midnight as it is. You're not the only one who needs to be well rested."

Taking her soft hand, he laced her arm through his and escorted her through the party. He didn't miss the fact that men seemed to keep their gaze on Mia a little longer than necessary…he knew the feeling of wanting to capture a mental picture of this beauty.

Mia, on the other hand, seemed oblivious to the attention.

"And here I thought all you Hollywood hotshots never slept," she went on, smiling up at him.

Those dark-as-night eyes could make a man forget any scruples he had. The sweet floral scent radiating off all that bare skin made his mouth water. If the woman was this potent after one evening, how would he survive the rest of the trip?

Dammit. He hated being vulnerable, and Mia was working her way fast and hard under his skin.

"I won't lie," he told her. "We do burn the midnight oil quite often. Which is why we need to sleep when we can."

As they stepped out into the warm night air, Bronson tasted the saltiness of the sea on his lips. He couldn't help but wonder if Mia would taste the same.

Yachts lined the docks and bobbed gently with the subtle ripples of the Mediterranean. Thousands of twinkling lights glistened off the black water, setting a romantic ambiance seen in movies.

Obviously, a realistic effect.

"This place is amazing." Mia snuggled closer to him as she looked out over the water. "I could live here and just stare at that gentle rolling tide all day."

"We have coastline at home, as well."

She looked back at him and tilted her head. "True, but there's something romantic and glamorous about Cannes. I love Hollywood, but it's all so…fake."

Bronson laughed. "Fake? You've never faked anything?"

"No," she said without hesitation. "What you see is what you get."

His eyes roamed over her, then landed back on her flawless face. "The exterior is perfect without faking anything. But what about on the inside? You've never lied? That's faking the truth. No?"

Mia looked back to the sea. "We all lie about something at some point, Bronson. It's human nature not to reveal the truth when a lie can benefit us."

Bronson stepped in front of her, keeping his hand on her arm. When she turned her gaze to face him, moonlight sparked off those deep, chocolate eyes. If he weren't careful, he'd fall into them and lose the battle he was fighting with himself.

"What are you faking now, Mia?" he whispered.

A soft breeze from the water lifted a tendril of her hair and sent it dancing. He tucked the strand behind her ear, stroking a finger down the side of her face, down her neck until her breath caught.

"I told you." She licked her lips, mocking Bronson because he wanted to be the one to lick that salty sea air off her parted mouth. "What you see is what you get."

"What I get, huh?" he asked with a slight grin.

Bronson slid his hand up her bare arm, cupped the back of her neck and captured her lips beneath his.

Perfect. Absolutely…perfect.

God, he'd been so right in believing her lips would taste amazing. Soft, giving. Mia may be holding a secret, but if it had anything to do with her sexuality, he'd just uncovered it. There was a passion brewing beneath this confident, yet private woman.

She wrapped her fingers around his biceps, whether to push him away or hold on as he continued assaulting her mouth he didn't know. But he wasn't going to stop unless she made him because one taste, just one, had him pulling her against him. His hands roamed up that bare back that had mocked him all evening. Damn this dress. He wanted it off her. Now.

With their bodies only separated by his tux shirt and thin layers of chiffon over her breasts, Bronson could feel the effect he had on her.

A snap and flash had him pulling back just in time to see a paparazzo running in the other direction.

Damn.

"Oh, God, did he…"

"Yeah." Bronson gritted his teeth, taking a step back to put some space between them. "He snapped our picture and now he's probably running back to whatever rag he works for."

Mia held a hand over her mouth, eyes wide as she stared back at him. "Oh, Bronson, I'm so sorry."

"Sorry because we kissed or sorry because we got caught?"

She smoothed that dangling strand of hair back. "Is that your way of finding out my feelings about what just happened? I'm not sorry we kissed. Surprised, but not sorry. I am sorry if what just happened ends up in the newspaper and causes more grief for your family in the press, especially with my recent scandal."

Her concern seemed genuine—but so had her French accent.

Bronson shrugged. "My body blocked your face, so as far as the media's concerned, you're a nameless woman."

But now that he'd had a sample, Bronson wanted the rest of what she had to offer.

Three

Nameless woman.

Mia wished those words from two nights ago still didn't cut right into her heart, but they did. Is that how Bronson saw her? Was he just kissing her as a prelude to a passing fling? How many women walked away from this Hollywood playboy on weak knees, nursing a broken heart?

God knew hers were still shaking from that toe-curling kiss. But would she just be a statistic when this week was all over? How flattering.

Mia touched up her lip gloss over lips that ached for more of Bronson's touch and examined herself in the ballroom's bathroom mirror. The short, deep plum dress with one shoulder bare and the other with a long, flowing sleeve made her feel just as sexy and feminine as the previous dresses.

Night three of the festival was no different than the others…except that she was aching even more for Bronson, and she knew she was every kind of a fool for feeling this way.

She was realistic, though. He may want her physically, but that's where their relationship ended. That didn't stop her from daydreaming, and their smoldering kiss certainly hadn't done a thing to diminish her attraction. Bronson Dane was every woman's walking fantasy, and her hormones were no different than those of any other female who'd had the fortunate opportunity to be close to the Hollywood powerhouse.

Mia smoothed a hand over her belly, trying to calm her jumbled nerves. Only a few more days and they would be back in Hollywood, and Bronson would be off to meetings about his next movie prospect.

She'd watched him charm actresses and build up actors' egos, though Mia knew it was just for leverage if he wanted them in a film one day. Hollywood was all about getting everything you wanted, no matter who you had to play to get it. And Bronson played the game like a pro.

But she doubted he needed to do all the charming. Bronson Dane was a force to be reckoned with in the industry. Turning down a chance to work with him would be an idiotic career move for anyone.

Mia smiled at an elderly woman and exited the bathroom. Just as she turned at the end of the hallway, she ran into Anthony Price.

"Mia." He pulled her into his strong arms for a friendly hug. "I thought I saw you the other night, but discounted the idea. I didn't know you'd be here."

She jerked back. "You can't do that. What if someone had taken a picture?" What if Bronson had seen them?

Anthony glanced around. "Paparazzi aren't allowed in here, but I do apologize. I was just shocked and happy to see you. Are you here with Olivia?"

Mia smiled at her previous employer. "And Bronson."

Anthony's smile dimmed. "Really. Do they—"

"I haven't said a word, Anthony." She knew he was nervous about opening a nearly forty-year-old secret and potentially ruining lives—she didn't blame him. "I told you I wouldn't reveal the secret and I keep my word."

"I know you do." He sighed. "I just haven't figured out how to handle this. I mean, after all these years, lives will be changed forever. Not only that, but with my situation at home…"

Glancing behind her, Mia offered a smile. "I know. I'm here for you any time you need me. Don't think because I'm not working for you that I'm not available to talk."

"I appreciate that, Mia." Anthony smiled. "I'm still trying to figure out why I let you go."

"Because your marriage is more important than your assistant," she reminded him. "You'll be just fine, Anthony. You both need some time. But I should get back to the party before Bronson starts looking for me or someone sees us. It certainly won't help your case."

"You're right. I can't afford to lose Charlotte. But it was so good to see you again."

"Perfect timing."

Mia jerked around at Bronson's deep voice. "Bronson."

"Don't let me interrupt," he told her, his gaze on Anthony. "I was wondering if you were okay, but now I see you are."

Why did she feel like she'd been caught doing something she shouldn't have? Damn. Could she not talk to a close friend without someone assuming something more sinister was going on?

Mia was smack dab in the middle of two of the most powerful men she knew. The air around them crackled with tension. Now that she could see them both up close, she studied their faces.

Yes, the resemblance was there. Subtle, but it was there.

Ironic that biological half brothers, raised in two separate families, could both grow up to be Hollywood moguls and totally despise each other.

"I didn't realize Mia was your date," Anthony told Bronson. "You're a lucky man."

Bronson's gaze narrowed. "Yes."

Mia couldn't handle the awkward silence. God, if she was this uncomfortable, she couldn't imagine how Anthony felt, having known the truth for the past six months.

When Anthony chose to reveal the secret to Olivia, he'd told Mia he would not cause a big scene and make more scandal than necessary. Even though he and Bronson despised each other, Anthony had always expressed his respect and admiration for the Grand Dane and wouldn't do anything to purposely hurt her. Though he would confront her, eventually. He had a lot of questions for her.

Well, Mia knew one thing. She didn't want these two together any longer. All they needed to do was have an argument about anything at all and news of it would be sent to every media outlet within moments—complete with pictures that would fuel the press even more.

She moved over to Bronson, placing a hand on his arm. "You ready? I could use some champagne."

The muscle in Bronson's jaw ticked. Mia gave a subtle tug on his arm.

"It was great to see you, Anthony," she said.

"You look beautiful, as always, Mia." Anthony leaned over and kissed Mia on the cheek. "I'm sure I'll see you again before the festival is over."

Mia smiled and, thank God, Bronson led her toward the

champagne fountains. Celebrities mingled, sipping drinks, laughing, and all Mia could think of was how hard her heart was pounding over being in the middle of Bronson and Anthony. Mercy, they were something remarkable to look at, but she certainly wouldn't want to be on the receiving end of either of their angry stares.

As long as she just focused on her job and let Anthony handle everything, she had nothing to worry about. Yes, she wanted to help blend these two broken siblings, but that was not her place. Because she knew—God did she know—how much damage could be done by letting a life-altering secret slip.

Mia stopped at the champagne fountain and turned to Bronson. "Relax."

His piercing blue gaze landed on her. "I'm relaxed."

"You were until you saw Anthony. Now you're shooting daggers."

"It's no secret that we don't get along," Bronson told her. He took a delicate flute and filled it with champagne. "Besides, I thought you two were finished. Or don't you care who sees you?"

"I worked for him. We're friends. That's the extent of our relationship." Mia took the drink he offered.

"You two looked cozy when I found you." Bronson lifted a brow, tilting his head. "And the media says otherwise."

Mia didn't even pretend not to know what he was talking about. Her eyes narrowed. "You should know you can't believe everything the Hollywood tabloids print. Why do you care anyway?"

Bronson shrugged, eyes roaming over the crowd. "None of my concern what you did with your ex-employer as long as it doesn't trickle over into my family."

His close-to-the-truth words nearly had her choking on

her champagne. Mia quickly composed herself as his eyes came back to settle on her.

"Nothing gets in the way of my job," she assured him. "I'm thrilled to be working for your mother."

His silence combined with his intense stare left her unsettled.

"There's something more, isn't there?" she asked. There had to be. Anger radiated off Bronson. "You look ready to—"

"Leave it alone, Mia."

His firm tone left no doubt he wasn't happy with her observation. There was something deeper than just not getting along on set, but Bronson was private and there's no way he would tell Mia…nor was it any of her business. Yet she couldn't help her curiosity.

"Why did my talking to Anthony get you so riled up?"

"No concern of yours." Bronson closed his eyes briefly, then opened them and settled them on her. "Just had a flashback of another time. Another place."

Another woman. The words hung in the air, just the same as if he'd said them. Jealousy from Bronson Dane was certainly not something she expected, but she had a strong feeling past and present were getting jumbled together.

"It's getting late," he told her. "I'll walk you to your room."

Mia handed her glass off to a passing waiter. "Of course."

Something had transpired between those two men, and more than likely no one knew about it but them. She certainly hadn't heard anything while working with Anthony…at least nothing out of the ordinary.

If Bronson was this angry now, she could only imagine how furious he would be once he found out Anthony was his older brother.

* * *

Bronson didn't know what he wanted more—to know what secret Mia and Anthony had been discussing or whether or not they'd been involved.

No. That was wrong. What he wanted most right now was Mia. Naked. Whatever had happened between her and Anthony in the past was irrelevant to what he wanted now. He refused to relive any part of the last relationship he'd had with a woman he'd trusted. Trusted her so much he'd been ready to spend his life with her and their child.

Their child. That turned out to be another lie.

Bronson rid his mind of that painful time and concentrated on something he understood. Lust. Good old-fashioned lust. He wanted the sexy, sultry Italian woman who'd taunted him with her radiant beauty, her teasing jasmine scent and the power she held over him.

Ushering Mia off the elevator, Bronson snaked his arm around her waist, guiding her toward her suite at the end of the wide hall.

Silence had accompanied them from the party, though the sexual tension had been apparent between them on the ride up. Now there was just one thing on his mind.

Mia pulled her key card from her small silver clutch and opened the door.

"Do you want to come in?"

And that was all the invitation he needed.

"Yes," he said before he palmed her face and pulled her hard against him.

This was what he'd fantasized about since seeing her wearing droplets. Desired since she'd come to Cannes and strolled into the lobby wearing that draped-back dress. But this dress, this one-shouldered number, would be so easy to peel off her. And he would be shedding her dress in a matter of seconds.

Right now, though, he concentrated on her mouth. Her perfect lips that gave all he took. The lips he'd ached for since he'd tasted them two long nights ago.

He backed her into the suite, her clutch falling from her grasp just as the door slammed behind them. Her hands clenched around his biceps and squeezed just as she let out a soft moan.

Bronson lifted his mouth just a fraction. "I've wanted you for days. Tell me you're not still with Anthony."

"I never have been," she assured him before she captured his mouth again.

Mia was just as hot and passionate as he'd anticipated, and even more so than the other night. Perhaps because they were behind a closed door now. And Bronson had every intention of taking advantage of this privacy. No paparazzi, no media. Pure, utter privacy.

He couldn't take in enough of her at once. He wanted her. Naked. Now.

He continued moving her into the room until the backs of her legs bumped into the decorative table in the living area. All power was lost, all control vanished. His mouth traveled down her jawline to her neck, from her bare shoulder and on to the top of the clingy dress.

Mia placed her hands behind her on the table and arched into him, offering herself up as if she'd been needing, craving this moment as much as he had.

He lifted his head and slid the thin material down her arm until she freed herself of the unwanted sleeve. An ache he didn't remember having in a long, long time encompassed every part of him. Taking the hem of her dress, he eased it up as Mia shifted from side to side to assist.

"I don't have protection with me," he told her, cursing himself for being ill-prepared.

"I have some in the cosmetic bag on the table behind you."

God bless a prepared woman. He shuffled through the bag in a hurry, found the foil wrapper and smacked it on the table next to Mia's hip.

She'd moved the dress farther up to her waist, giving him more than a glimpse of what she wore beneath.

"Beautiful," he whispered as his eyes landed on the small scrap of lace in the same shade of purple as her dress. He slid the garment down her toned legs and over the stilettos. The fantasy shoes had to stay.

"You don't know how much you've driven me crazy." Bronson made quick work of his pants while Mia nipped along his jawline.

"Then kiss me because I'm going just as crazy waiting."

She scooted to the edge of the table as he donned protection. Her long legs wrapped around his waist and he lost no time in taking her.

Yes…yes. Her body moved perfectly against his, and Bronson had to work to keep from being too rough, too fast. He wanted this feeling of euphoria to last. The anticipation building up to this paled in comparison to having Mia draped all around him.

He realized then that the past two days had all been foreplay leading up to this moment. And each one of those stepping-stones, from the subtle touches to the harmless flirting, was mild when he had Mia right where he wanted her.

With her body wrapped around his, Bronson set the rhythm, pleased when an audible sigh escaped her full, moist lips.

It was those lips that had driven him crazy. Hell, the entire package made him feel like a horny teenager, but those lips mocked him when they smiled, when they talked. When they moaned.

Bronson kept the pace fast because nothing, absolutely nothing could slow him down now. He feasted on Mia's mouth. She grabbed hold of his shoulders, gripping the tux shirt he still wore because being inside her had taken precedence over being fully undressed.

Sweat drenched the skin beneath his shirt, and a fine sheen covered Mia's shoulders as he moved his lips down to one freed breast.

He didn't care that this was his mother's assistant, didn't care if she'd had or hadn't had a relationship with Anthony. All Bronson knew was that he wanted this woman, and what he wanted, he took. And Mia, the intriguing, dark-eyed beauty, had been onboard from the first kiss.

When her body shivered, shook, Bronson stopped holding back and let go. As they crested together, he knew this was not a one-time thing.

When their trembling ceased, Mia opened her eyes and smiled. "I have to say, I like how you walk me to my room."

Bronson nipped at her swollen, moist lips. "I should warn you: I intend to do this again as soon as I recover."

Trembling fingers toyed with the buttons on his shirt. "Maybe we could be skin to skin this time."

Anticipation rippled through him. "Absolutely."

No, Bronson didn't care that Mia was his mother's assistant, didn't care that he didn't trust her. And he sure as hell didn't care if she was now or ever had been involved with Anthony Price.

Because he wasn't getting his heart involved with anyone ever again. Not after his last relationship. His ex-fiancée had walked away after miscarrying a child he'd thought was his.

His ex-fiancée had met Anthony on a movie set, where she'd been the makeup artist, ironically the same way Bronson had met her. When Bronson and she began arguing after the death of the baby, and their relationship became strained, she'd thrown the supposed affair in his face once she'd walked out on him.

So, no, there was no love lost between Anthony and him. And any potential for future relationships was completely destroyed after that whole fiasco.

Lust and sex. That's all Bronson had room for in his life, and the very naked woman in his arms would fill that void nicely.

Four

Six weeks later...

What had she eaten?

Mia groaned. Closing her eyes, she let her head fall back against the plush sofa cushions. In the seven months she'd worked for Olivia, never once had she asked for a day, or even an hour, off. But today there was absolutely no way she could've made it through the afternoon without falling over or running to the bathroom and hugging the commode—not qualities a personal assistant to the Grand Dane should possess.

Olivia had taken pity on her and sent her home, with the promise Mia would call if she felt worse or needed anything at all. Mia would've promised anything to anyone if it meant she could crawl back onto her comfy sofa and lie perfectly still. Why did the house keep shifting?

Yeah, there was no way at all she could've kept up with the fast-paced, never-tiring Olivia Dane. Not today.

With the majority of her work on her laptop, she was just fine right here in her own living room. Well, she would be fine if the room would stop tilting and her stomach would stop rolling. Seriously, all she'd had for dinner the previous night was a piece of baked fish and some steamed veggies. Nothing at all to prove fatal, yet death was surely knocking at her door because concentrating on these fan emails was taking the last bit of energy she had.

Mia lifted her head and clicked on another email with a sigh. The message, like hundreds of others, wanted to know when Bronson would produce a film with his mother playing the lead role. The public loved this close-knit Hollywood family, and the fact that the Grand Dane and the best producer in the business hadn't worked together yet kept people interested.

Why did everything circle back to Bronson? In the six weeks since he'd left Cannes to go on a business trip for his next film, she hadn't heard a word from him. She'd been in the room once when he'd called to chat with his mother, but that was as close as she came to the man who'd given her the most spine-tingling night of her life.

Obviously, he'd been able to move on, so why was she still hanging on to the memories of his touch, his kiss? His taste. She lived in Hollywood. Sexual partners came and went. Unfortunately, sex had always meant more to Mia that just a casual coupling.

But, she reminded herself, he'd stressed that he didn't want anything personal, and she completely understood. For one night of passion with Hollywood's hottest bachelor, she'd put her moral compass aside and taken one for the team.

Though deep down, there was that little girl inside her

who wished for the old Hollywood fairy tale, the handsome man to sweep her off her feet, the mansion where they'd live happily ever after. Of course she'd keep all her wishes and dreams to herself, but she couldn't help the fantasies that flitted through her mind.

Unfortunately this was Hollywood. Unfulfilled fantasies were everywhere. But she didn't care if wanting her dreams to become reality made her naive. She'd continue to be a hopeless romantic.

She clasped the locket around her neck, the image of her parents' picture inside flooding her mind. They'd chased their dreams when they'd come to America from Italy. So what if she was a dreamer? That only made her work harder for what she wanted. And a part of her did want Bronson. Granted, she didn't know him that well, but she'd like to get to know him better. He'd been so attentive, so giving with his affection, not to mention he'd been a true gentleman the entire week they'd spent together.

But had she seriously thought Bronson would sleep with her, find himself falling madly in love and they'd ride off into the sunset in a town that was full of lies and deceit? Even couples who'd been married for a number of years seemed to fall into the bottomless pit of divorce.

And why was she wasting a workday fantasizing about weddings, divorces and Bronson's thrilling touch?

Mia's hands flew across the keyboard as she replied to the interested fan. There was nothing in the works for Olivia and Bronson, but that didn't mean it wasn't a possibility. And Mia knew the two would love to work on a film together, they just hadn't found the right one—or so she'd been told.

This was the part of her job she dearly loved—hearing from all the people around the world who reminisced about old Grand Dane movies and still enjoyed seeing her on the big screen with the hottest up-and-coming young stars. No doubt about it—when Olivia Dane made an entrance on to the screen, the audience loved her. No one could ever overshadow her beauty, class or intelligence. She reigned supreme even over today's hottest stars.

As she read more fan mail exuding love for this success-ful, bonded family, guilt washed over her.

When would Anthony tell Olivia he knew the truth? On one hand, Mia wanted it to be out in the open so she didn't have to hoard all this guilt. But, on the other hand, once the truth was out, how many lives would be ruined? Would the Danes be able to move on? They were such a tight-knit family and had lived through minor scandals, but something of this magnitude could cause tremendous up-heaval. Anthony and Bronson already loathed each other. Informing Bronson they were brothers would surely prove to only drive that hatred to a deeper level.

And ruining Olivia's flawless image wouldn't solve any-thing.

Mia's stomach churned again. Between the constant fear of how these two families would cope with a forty-year-old secret and whatever stomach bug she'd picked up, Mia was ready to crawl back into bed and call it a day. Unfor-tunately, it was only ten in the morning and she still had about fifty more emails to get to and some phone calls to return for Olivia's TV talk show appearances to promote the new movie she had a cameo in. No rest for the dying.

Just as she opened another email, the doorbell sounded throughout the cottage. *Cottage* was a silly word for the five-thousand-square-foot guesthouse, complete with its own swimming pool, hot tub and movie room with a floor-to-ceiling movie screen. However, compared to the main house, at twenty-two-thousand square feet, this was defi-nitely a cottage.

Mia came to her feet, thankful the room had stopped tilting for the time being, glanced down to her less-than-professional attire and shrugged. She'd changed into something more comfortable when Olivia had sent her home and hadn't expected to see anyone else today.

Oh, well. More than likely if it wasn't Olivia herself, then she'd sent one of the staff to check on her. Mia loved that Olivia cared for her in that motherly way…a way her own mother never had the chance to. She only prayed the cook hadn't brought food, as Olivia had suggested. The thought sent her stomach revolting—again.

The cool tile beneath her feet as she crossed the foyer felt refreshing, considering she was getting a bit light-headed again. Maybe she needed to crank up the AC or get a cool cloth for her head.

Mia twisted the lock and opened her door to see Bronson in all his gorgeous glory bathed in the sunlight falling over his shoulder. With his California tan, styled "messy" hair, green polo and dark designer jeans, he looked every bit of perfect. So opposite her. Oh, wait, she had the messy hair, just not in the stylish way he sported it. No, hers was more of the get-out-of-my-face-because-I'm-going-to-be-sick mess in a topknot with stray pieces hanging down.

"I called up to the house. Mom told me you were sick," Bronson said, leaning against her doorjamb. "Is there anything you need?"

Really? He'd rushed here after not a word in weeks? A phone call would've proved just fine and then she wouldn't have to worry about how deathly she looked while he, as usual, looked drop-dead sexy. If he hadn't put their sexual encounter out of his mind already, one look at her would surely have him running for the next starlet.

"Mia. Do you need anything?" he asked again.

Yeah, for him to leave and only return when her makeup

was on, her hair was done and her breath couldn't be used as a weapon.

"I'm good." She smiled. "Did you come over just to see how I was?"

Bronson shrugged. "I just got back into town a couple days ago and I was going to stop by to see you anyway."

"Really?" Considering the six-week gap since they last saw each other, she was a little skeptical. "Why?"

"Honestly?"

Mia grabbed the edge of the door for some stability and lifted a brow. Yeah, she wouldn't mind a little honesty from the man she'd slept with and couldn't get out of her mind.

Bronson threw her that billion-dollar, white-tooth smile. "I wanted to see you again. I was hoping for dinner at my place, but if you're sick, we can postpone."

If she'd had the energy to jump up and down, she probably would have. Even the giddy girl inside her was wiped out this morning.

"I haven't even agreed to see you again and you're already making plans to postpone?" she asked. "My, my. Awfully full of yourself."

Reaching into his back pocket, he whipped out a well-worn, folded-up tabloid.

Mia took it, unfolded it and saw the cover. A cover with the two of them in a heated embrace, kissing. Their first kiss that some paparazzo schmuck had captured and exploited. Not only was that picture blown up as the main feature, but there were also smaller pictures surrounding the perimeter. Snapshots from the red carpet, one picture of the two of them when they'd been waiting to meet with his mother for lunch—but, of course, Olivia wasn't in the photo.

The headline read, "DANE'S NEW LEADING LADY?" She'd seen these images and more intrusive headlines on the internet, but they'd only popped up for a few days. More Hollywood drama had unfolded since then, and their little week in Cannes had been pushed aside.

Mia's eyes darted to Bronson. "Why would this make you so confident I'd want to see you again? Aren't you the one who wanted to keep things to that one night?"

Bronson's bright baby blues roamed over her, heating her and making her feel just a wee bit better. "I do prefer simple, but after I saw these pictures, I knew I needed to see you again. The way you're looking at me, the way we look kissing—it's hard to deny that there's some real chemistry between us, Mia. And the camera picks up everything."

Shivers rippled one after another through her body as she slapped the the tabloid down onto the small table by the door. "In most of these we're looking at each other. I'd say the chemistry isn't completely one-sided."

"As I said, the camera picks up everything." One corner of his kissable mouth tilted. "Which is why I'd like to see you again."

And today she was not feeling, or looking, her best. Was this fate's way of telling her to take the night she had and move on without getting too involved with this man? She did know a secret that would crumble the solid foundation his world was built upon. On the other hand, she wanted to see this charming, sexy man again, away from the romantic, alluring ambiance of Cannes. She wanted to see if this chemistry was real.

"I'll call later to check on you," he told her. "If you're feeling up to it, I've got a great dinner planned."

Mia's eyes widened. "You're going to cook?"

"I've been banned from my own kitchen because I'm so terrible at cooking. But I assure you my chef will prepare a feast you'll never forget." His eyes grew dark, and a smile curved at his lips. "But my staff will have the night off when you're there. I promise you my undivided attention. If you're not feeling well, we can reschedule. Tomorrow?"

"No, I'll be fine. I'm sure I just need to rest."

Bronson stepped over the threshold, forcing her to take a step back. His finger trailed down her cheek, as if she needed a reminder of how spine-tingling his touches were. Those touches had driven her mad in Cannes, and she couldn't wait for an encore. Please, God, let her feel better after a nap and some Pepto.

"You look a bit pale." His brows drew together. "We'll do it tomorrow."

Great, here she'd been thinking of the last time he'd touched her with those talented hands and he was commenting on how deathly she looked. Didn't she just reek sex appeal?

His hand came back to her forehead and she swatted him away, but not before his palm rested over her head and cheek.

"Really, Bronson, I'm not in the mood to play doctor-patient. Tomorrow I'll feel better and we can have that dinner at your place. Maybe I'll bring my stethoscope."

A grin tugged at the corner of his mouth. "I'd like nothing more than to see your bedside manner again, but let's get you feeling better. Okay?"

"Fine," she agreed. "Tomorrow. I'll be there."

"I'll pick you up," he told her. "Five o'clock."

He turned and strolled back to his sleek, black sports car, leaving her standing in her doorway. That man had whipped back into her life as fast as he'd left and here she was panting after him just like the last time.

Oh, well. She didn't care what she looked like, she only cared about being with Bronson again because that man held more arousing power in his lips and fingertips than most men held in their entire bodies.

She was not going to let Anthony's secret or this stupid virus keep her from seeing him tomorrow. Because there was no way she would miss a repeat of the Cannes event. If Bronson had thought of her since then—and he obviously had or he wouldn't be carrying around that tabloid—then he wanted her just as much as she wanted him.

Dinner invite to his place? That just screamed for her to wear her best lingerie.

Bronson dove headfirst into his Olympic-size pool. Getting his laps in not only kept him in great shape, but allowed him to unwind after a long day. One of his favorite places in this Beverly Hills home was the pool. And each time he came home from business, he spent his evenings here. Even when the sun set and the stars came out twinkling, he found the water refreshing and could reflect on the happenings in his life.

And right now Mia Spinelli was happening in a big way.

Never before had a woman distracted him from his work. But in the weeks since the one they'd shared in Cannes, she'd done just that.

The first tabloid he'd seen nearly had him cringing, but that was just a knee-jerk reaction to the ever-looming media. Once he looked more closely at the picture, or *pictures*, rather, he'd seen something he couldn't deny. He wasn't lying when he'd told her the camera picks up everything.

Bronson pushed off the concrete wall and began the backstroke. The paparazzo had captured that first kiss at just the right moment and just the right angle to keep Mia's face a mystery. More pictures had shown her with her back to the camera, and that's when he'd noticed just how he'd been looking at her.

With lust. Pure and simple. He couldn't deny the attraction, and since he'd had her that's all he'd been able to think of. Luckily, his business trip hadn't taken as long as he'd thought and now he could concentrate on luring the seductive Mia into his bed once more.

Beyond that, he needed to keep an eye on her because he still wasn't convinced that she wasn't hiding something or out to benefit from working with his rival and now his mother.

As he came to rest with his arms on the side of the pool, Bronson vowed if Mia was hiding something, or working some angle, he'd uncover it…and, along the way, uncover her.

The next morning came with a vengeance as Mia threw back her covers and raced to the bathroom.

Just in time.

Good grief. She'd been fine yesterday afternoon and evening. Why was she feeling this way for the second morning in a row?

Mia's hands froze as she reached to flush the commode. Oh, no. No. This timing had to be coincidental. Fate wouldn't be this cruel to her…would it?

Easing back on her heels, her mind raced, calculating the date.

Oh, God.

Her period had always been on an odd cycle, but she'd never gone this long without one. Her eyes immediately went to her stomach. Surely there wasn't a baby growing inside her. She refused to believe it. Unfortunately, the facts were piling up fast, leaving her heart beating heavy against her chest, giving her a whole new reason to be nauseous.

Damn, she didn't have one of those at-home pregnancy tests on hand. She never thought she'd need one. But even if she ran out and bought one, were they 100 percent accurate? She had no clue what to do here. She'd never found herself in this predicament.

She needed to get to the doctor. Now. She needed to know the truth.

On shaky legs and with her thoughts moving through her mind faster than she could process them, Mia washed her face, brushed her teeth and threw on a strapless yellow sundress and flip-flops.

Grabbing her keys and handbag, she raced to the attached garage, pulling her cell out of her purse. By the time she got in her car, the receptionist told her they could do a walk-in test, no appointment needed. Thank God. She only hoped her sickness eased off long enough for her to find out the results.

Wait, shouldn't she be hoping for a negative test? An upset stomach was the least of her worries right now.

Mia raced down palm-lined streets, never more afraid or eager to go to the doctor. Once this scare was behind her, she could focus on her dinner with Bronson tonight and everything that went along with it.

But this night could have a totally different outcome if the pregnancy test came back positive.

Another scandal with her name all over it was the last thing she wanted. She was still trying to recover from the media painting her as the "other woman" in Anthony's marriage. Damn the paparazzi for adding to the already growing personal issues for Anthony and his wife. Not to mention the lies they made up about her all for the sake of a story.

Mia pulled into a parking spot on the street and tried not to run to the door, but a brisk walk was absolutely necessary. After entering the cool, air-conditioned building, Mia took the elevator to the third floor where her doctor's office was located, and thankfully had weekend hours.

She entered the carpeted waiting room and signed in on the walk-in tablet. In no time a nurse called her name and Mia started feeling queasy all over again. She could do this. She had to know.

Thirty minutes later when Mia stumbled out of the office, she rested against the wall in the empty hallway, trying to fathom what her life would be like now.

Because in thirty-four weeks, she and Bronson were going to have a baby.

Scandal with a Hollywood Hotshot: Take Two.

Five

Mia wanted nothing more than to forget the date with Bronson and hide in her house for the duration of her pregnancy.

Her pregnancy. She never thought those words would come to her mind when she wasn't in love, wasn't married and wasn't planning for a baby. But there was nothing she could do now except move forward and be upfront and honest with Bronson. And she would have to tell him… sooner rather than later.

But no matter how Bronson reacted, she wouldn't think of this baby as a mistake or a burden. The baby didn't ask to be conceived by two people who couldn't control their emotions.

Talk about a mood spoiler. Mia didn't put on her ugliest, lounge-around-the-house bra and panties, but her plans for her best lingerie were swiftly abandoned. After she dropped this bombshell tonight, she seriously doubted

Bronson would want to see how she filled out her newest Victoria's Secret purchase. And why was she even having those thoughts? That's the same path of destruction that had gotten her in this situation.

Dammit, they'd used a condom.

If she thought she'd been nervous before she found out the results, that anxiety was nothing compared to the thought of telling Bronson that he was going to be a father. She recalled that he'd been engaged before and they'd been expecting a baby, but his ex-fiancée had miscarried. What would he feel now? How would he react to another baby?

She'd rehearsed in her head over and over just the right way to say it, but was there really a right way to upend someone's life? She certainly wasn't his fiancée, was barely his lover. So how were they going to handle this arrangement?

Not only that, this scandal would send the media into another feeding frenzy. First she's accused of sleeping with Anthony and breaking up his marriage, and now she's carrying Bronson's child.

Just wait until the media circus discovered the two men were brothers. Wouldn't that just burn up the phone lines from reporter to reporter? She didn't want to even think about the headlines surrounding her when that time came.

Mia nearly laughed at the irony. Now she knew two secrets that would surely have Bronson reevaluating life and the hand it dealt him.

When her doorbell rang, she jumped. With a calming breath and a quick prayer, Mia left the comfort of her bedroom, smoothed a hand down her blue halter dress and went to answer the door.

She greeted Bronson with a smile, but just seeing him caused an ache she hadn't expected. She truly cared what he would do and say, but she was especially interested to see how he would handle this news emotionally, because soon another bomb would drop in his life that was just as big as him being a father.

His eyes raked over her. "You have no idea how glad I am we aren't going out. You look amazing."

Mia swallowed the lump of guilt and tamped down the arousal from his words. "Thank you."

She closed the door behind her and accepted his hand as he led her to his black luxury SUV. Just as she grabbed for the handle, he reached around her and opened the door. But before she could climb in, he took her shoulders and turned her back against the side of the car.

"I can't wait any longer for a sample."

Bronson's lips came down on hers and Mia had no choice but to melt into him. His hands settled on her waist as he pulled her lower body against his. With a grip on his muscular biceps, Mia returned the kiss with all the passion she had because—baby or no baby—she still craved this man like no other.

Obviously, their time apart hadn't banished her from his mind. In a sense she was thrilled that the ever-present attraction wasn't one-sided, but his feelings were likely going to change when he learned about the baby.

Bronson stepped back. "We may have to have the main course first."

Mia didn't even have to ask—she knew the main course was *not* something his chef had whipped up in the kitchen.

She climbed up into the SUV, sighing when he closed her door. She could do this. Millions of women broke the news of pregnancy all the time. Once the secret was out in the open, they'd be able to move on and deal with the consequences of their night together.

Bronson climbed in and brought the engine to life. When they were on the freeway headed to his Beverly Hills mansion, he took hold of her hand. "Everything okay? You seem awfully quiet."

"Everything's fine," she told him, nerves growing stronger with each passing second. "Just ready to relax."

Yeah, as if that were possible.

"You're not still feeling sick are you? Did that pass?"

Mia suppressed the groan. "It passed." *But it'll be back in the morning.*

"Great, because my cook made the most amazing Alfredo lasagna with a freshly tossed salad and vinaigrette dressing. I also have Italian bread and tiramisu for dessert."

Impressed, Mia smiled. "Wow. You know I'm Italian, right? I'm a harsh critic."

He gave her hand a gentle squeeze and laughed. "I always aim to please, Mia, and I know you'll enjoy everything I have in store for this evening."

The Mia who'd initially agreed to come have dinner with him would no doubt enjoy everything he had to offer. The pregnant, shocked, petrified Mia...not as eager. She had a feeling a lot of harsh words might be spoken and feelings would be hurt before the end of the night.

But when did she announce the news? Before dinner when they'd barely had a chance to talk? Or after when he'd no doubt put those seductive moves on her?

Definitely between the dinner and before the moves, because Mia knew once he started roaming those talented hands over her body, she'd be done. And it would be very, very wrong to take advantage of the situation when she had information that would almost certainly change the mood.

But would he be excited about the baby, about another Dane entering the dynasty? Mia hadn't paid that much attention to the press when he'd been engaged and lost a baby before, since she'd worked for Anthony at that time. But she knew a little bit about Bronson. He was a family man, and that loss of a child had to have nearly destroyed him. How would he accept another baby? And Mia couldn't help but selfishly wonder where she factored into this equation.

As they pulled into his gated drive, Bronson punched in a code and the lacey gates, complete with wrought-iron initials, parted and slid to either side of the drive.

She didn't know what to expect of Bronson's house, maybe a version of his mother's in that sleek white, Mediterranean style. But Bronson's three-story home exuded masculinity with the dark brick and large windows on each floor. Tall palms surrounded the curved home with a circle drive. No frilly flowers for him. Everything was green, lush and thriving.

"Your home is beautiful, Bronson."

He pulled into the attached four-car garage, closing the door behind them, sending them into darkness. "I'm not here often enough to enjoy it, but I do love it."

Would she be too forward if she asked about someday filling a home this large with a wife and children? Probably not the way to approach the topic of her pregnancy. God, she just had to say it. Once the words were out, they could deal with it, but her courage had failed to accompany her tonight.

She toyed with the locket around her neck, as if to draw strength from the two loving people pictured inside.

They exited the car and Bronson led her into the house through the kitchen any chef would die to just spend one day in—four built-in stoves, a brick pizza oven, three sinks mounted beneath gray concrete countertops. Dark mahogany cabinets made the large space look and feel masculine.

"Do you know what I'd do to have a kitchen like this?" she asked, running her fingertips along the grooved edges of the counter. "I love to cook in my spare time. I think I subscribe to every cooking magazine there is. With all this counter space, the stoves… My mind is working overtime."

Bronson tossed his keys onto the counter. "Feel free to come over anytime and let that imagination run wild. I'm a disaster in the kitchen."

She doubted that invite would last once she told him about the baby. Amazing how quick she'd gotten used to saying the words in her head without feeling the need to scream or cry. But they were going to have a baby, so why worry about something she couldn't change?

"Everything smells delicious," she told him. "Is it going to taste just as good?"

Bronson extended his hand toward the open eating area at the end of the kitchen. "Let's go find out."

She smiled at the round black table with high-back chairs, a simple white orchid in a slender glass vase and bright white plates waiting for the meal.

"Table for two?" she asked, throwing a smile over her shoulder. "You did go all out, didn't you? Or should I say your chef did."

Bronson pulled a chair out for her, brushed her hair from her shoulder and placed a gentle, tingling kiss right below her ear. "I may not have made the meal, but the rest is all me. I never need help impressing a woman."

Excitement mixed with guilt curled low in her belly. "Is that what you're trying to do? Impress me?"

"How am I doing?"

Exceptional. Wonderful. Perfect.

And why couldn't this night end the way she wanted, ached for it to? Why couldn't she have discovered the pregnancy tomorrow? Just one more night with him would've fulfilled her fantasies for years to come. Because she knew, once she dropped this bombshell, that would kill anything that had sparked weeks ago.

"Doing well so far," she told him, easing down into the chair.

Bronson brought over two full bowls of salad with dressing and fresh bread. Mia couldn't taste much, not for the secret on the tip of her tongue. She was a fraud, a liar. The kind of woman she despised.

Finally, she dropped her freshly buttered bread back onto the plate. "I can't do this."

With his fork halfway to his mouth, Bronson froze, eyes coming up to meet hers. "I'm sorry?"

Unable to stay seated any longer, Mia came to her feet and stood behind her chair, gripping the back. "I can't sit here and pretend this is going to go somewhere when I know it can't."

Bronson's fork clattered to his salad bowl. "What are you talking about, Mia? Are you having second thoughts about spending the evening with me?"

"Not at all, but you may have second thoughts about me when I tell you that…"

God, it was so much harder to say the words out loud, instead of just in her head. She'd never spoken them before and now that she was ready…well, she wasn't ready.

Bronson came to his feet, too, crossed to her and took her hands. "Come into the living room. You look like you're ready to pass out."

Funny, that's exactly how she felt and it had nothing to do with the morning sickness she'd been having.

Bronson led her to one of the two oversized leather sofas. She eased down, praying to find the right words, praying he wouldn't treat her differently. Praying he'd accept this baby.

And in all honesty, that's what everything boiled down to. With her background of foster homes and an unstable lifestyle, she just wanted this baby to be accepted and loved by Bronson. If he didn't love her, that was fine, but this baby didn't deserve to be shunned or kept from knowing his family.

He took a seat next to her, grabbing hold of one of her hands and bringing it to his lips. "Did something happen? Yesterday you seemed fine when we discussed our dinner date."

"That's because yesterday I was fine." Other than morning sickness. "And I'm fine today." Other than the morning sickness. "It's just my life has changed drastically since you saw me last."

His eyes roamed over her body and back up to her face. "You look the same. What is it?"

"I'm pregnant."

There, the words were out in the open and the world hadn't stopped spinning. Well, hers hadn't. She couldn't say the same for Bronson, who had just gone a shade paler.

"Pregnant?" he repeated.

Mia nodded slowly, afraid of what he'd say or do next.

"Now I understand why you're hesitant to be here with me." He came to his feet, as if he were afraid to sit next to her, touch her hand as he was. "Have you told the father? I mean, you two obviously aren't still involved or you wouldn't have agreed to come here, right?"

Mia placed an arm around her abdomen, trying to keep the hurt from seeping in even more. He didn't understand what she was saying. She'd never thought of that scenario when she'd rehearsed all of this in her head.

"Actually, we are still somewhat involved," she told him, looking up because she had to say this to his face and be brave. "You're the father, Bronson."

Six

Bronson heard the words, but he couldn't believe life could be this cruel. Another woman, another baby flashed through his mind and along with that came the hurt and betrayal he'd worked so hard to bury.

"I'm not the father, Mia."

Mia jerked, eyes wide. "Excuse me?"

Bronson shoved his hands in his pockets. "I believe you're pregnant, but I'm not the father. We used protection." And then he remembered and that pit in his stomach deepened. "*Your* condoms."

In an instant, she was on her feet, standing mere inches from him. "Are you implying I did this on purpose? Do you remember that night? Do you remember how I said good night and it was you who kissed me? You who backed me into the room and hiked up my dress?"

Bronson remembered…all too well, in fact. He remembered the rush to get her dress off, the rush as he fumbled with the condom and the pleasure he'd experienced like no other.

All the accusations surrounding her and Anthony flashed through his mind. How she'd supposedly broken up his marriage, how their affair had lasted several years.

"I know how it went down, Mia." Nausea threatened to overtake him, but he couldn't back down. "We used your condoms and now you're pregnant. Pretty coincidental, don't you think?"

In a flash, her palm connected with his cheek. The sting didn't even compare to the spearing pain running through him. He couldn't handle another baby that wasn't his. He could not, would not go down this path again. Nor would he be trapped, if somehow he really was the father, into a relationship or blackmailed for money.

"You expect me to take your word about something this serious?" he asked, rubbing his jaw.

Was that her angle? Was she trying to get money so she didn't have to work or so she could get into some headlines?

God, either scenario was a mess and fodder for all the gossip rags. He didn't know her angle, didn't care. His attorney would eat her alive and hopefully they would keep this insane accusation out of the media's hands.

How the hell had he let his guard down so fast, so easily with this woman? He'd wanted to stay close because he didn't trust her. Damn. How had his plan so completely backfired? Now he certainly didn't trust her.

"What is your angle, Mia?" Bronson crossed his arms over his chest, narrowing his eyes at her. He may as well be direct. "Was this your plan all along? To trap me? Does Anthony know you're pregnant, supposedly with my child?"

Mia stepped back. "Anthony? Why would I tell him? You're the first person I've told."

He had a hard time believing that. "You two looked pretty cozy when I found you together in Cannes. How do I know the baby isn't his?"

"How dare you? I am not a liar and I am not out to trap you into anything. I'm laying all the facts out there so we can deal with this baby who didn't ask to be brought into this world and I will not…"

Her words ended on a very persuasive hiccup as tears filled her eyes. She spun around, dropping her head to her chest.

Wow. Maybe he should cast her in his next film. She was damn convincing, but he wasn't falling for any of her theatrics.

"I want a DNA test as soon as possible," he told her. "I've been down this road before, Mia, and it didn't end well for me. Though I'm sure you already knew about the baby I lost."

Mia turned back to him, wiping her damp cheeks. "I do remember hearing about your ex-fiancée who lost the baby. I'm so sorry about that, but I assure you I love this baby already and will do everything to keep it safe."

Her soft tone made him want to believe she was truly sorry, but still, he didn't want to revisit the past with his ex-fiancée and the baby that ended up not being his, and he sure as hell didn't want to be living this nightmare again.

"I won't go through this again, Mia. I won't start a family with a woman I can't trust."

Mia's face paled at his words. "I'm just as shocked and scared as you. I never intended to get pregnant. If you don't want to be part of this child's life, that's your loss. But I will love this child and I will provide for it with or without your help. I've been alone my entire life. I'm used to it."

A sliver of Bronson wanted to believe this baby was his. Though he wasn't in love with Mia, he'd always wanted children to carry on the Dane dynasty, a wife to love. He wanted what his parents had had before his father's death.

But he had to be realistic. Mia probably saw this as her way to extort money from him, even if she claimed to not want part of his fortune.

"I won't pay you anything until I know for sure who this baby belongs to," he told her, not caring one bit that she looked like she was on the verge of tears again.

"I would never ask for anything from you," she said through gritted teeth. "I thought you should know, but if this is the attitude you're going to take, I don't even want you in my baby's life. We deserve better."

A psychological ploy used many times by thousands of women to trap the man into giving in. He wasn't falling for it. Now more than ever he needed to stay close to figure out exactly what her angle was.

"I assure you, Mia, if this baby's mine, I will be part of his life." He stepped closer to the woman who drove him insane on so many levels. "And if this baby's mine, whether I like it or not, I will be part of your life. Count on it."

Mia's lips thinned. "I don't want you in my life. Not after the accusations you've just hurled at me. I would never lie about something as serious as a baby. And I assure you, I haven't been with another man in over a year and, no, it was not Anthony. He was my employer and friend, that's all."

Yet again, she sounded and looked so convincing. And there was that part of him that wanted to believe her. He didn't even want to think of Anthony Price's hands on her willowy, soft body. Didn't want to think of another man's baby growing inside her. Not that he wanted a baby with her, either. Other than the sexual, physical attraction, what did they have in common?

Sure, before this bombshell, he'd considered seeing where that attraction could lead. But now...

Dammit. Why? Just...why?

Mia moved past him, charging back to the kitchen.

"Where are you going?" he asked, following her.

"To call a cab." She pulled her cell from the purse she'd left on the center island. "I think it's best if we both cool down and think rationally before talking about this again."

"I'll drive you home." He took the cell from her hand and hit the End button. "There's no need to call a cab. The paparazzi would get wind of your leaving here in tears and who knows what story they'd make up."

Mia stared at him, her face red from crying, her makeup smeared in one corner of her eye. And she was still beautiful. Alluring and simple all in one. But the most important question was, Was she a first-class liar who'd set out to trap him?

Only time would tell.

The pain sliced through her. Agony, frustration, despair. Even a week after dropping the news on Bronson, she still had that sickening pit in her stomach.

Mia curled up on her four-poster bed, refusing to cry. Expecting a child should be a joyous time in every woman's life, but this moment was anything but joyous.

Toying with the bronze beading on her comforter, Mia thought about the life growing inside her. Most women ran to their mothers for advice, or a sister or best friend. Who did she have? Seriously? She'd purposely engrossed herself in work so she could forget that she'd never had anyone in her life who cared...other than her parents, who'd died when she'd been only five years old. Her few friends had busy lives of their own. Too busy to call and share the news or borrow a shoulder to cry on.

Never before had being alone bothered her; she actually enjoyed being independent. But now, when her life was taking a dramatically sharp turn, she truly wished she had someone.

She hadn't expected Bronson to take the news well, but to accuse her of sabotaging the condom to trap him? That was beyond absurd. Once Bronson calmed down and could think rationally, would he believe her? Would Olivia and Victoria be happy or just as skeptical?

Oh, God. Would Olivia still let her remain in such a personal, intimate position? She needed this job, especially now with a baby coming—no way would she take any money from Bronson. That certainly wasn't the reason she'd told him.

No, she'd told him out of consideration and, dammit, because it was the right thing to do. So why was she allowing all this guilt to consume her?

Her blood pressure soared once again at the thought of his believing the worst. But stepping back and looking at it from his point of view, she could somewhat understand how he'd distrust her. They had used a condom—her condom—and he really didn't know her.

But the accusations he threw at her still cut deep. She prided herself on honesty and built her life on always telling the truth. Of course, that was before she saw the damning, life-altering file on Anthony's desk mere days before she started working for Olivia.

On a groan, Mia rolled onto her back and stared up at the ceiling. Her locket slid around her neck and tickled her ear.

Why did her life have to end up so complicated? Why couldn't she be like millions of other women who felt the joy and elation of having a baby? She'd always fantasized about telling the man of her dreams he would be a daddy. Now all her fantasies were shot.

But what did she expect, going to bed with a man she barely knew? Karma surely wasn't this cruel. She hadn't wanted any personal involvement with Bronson, especially until the secret of his illegitimate brother came out, and now she'd thrown herself smack dab in the center of his life—whether he wanted to admit it or not.

Mia glanced over at her clock and knew she couldn't avoid the inevitable. Monday morning came too fast, and now she had to get ready to head to the main house, spend the entire day with Olivia and pretend she wasn't hiding two major secrets from this woman.

As she made her way to her adjoining bath, Mia figured she deserved the good pity party she'd thrown for herself all weekend, but now it was time to take charge and stand strong. This was her life, she was bringing a baby into it and she needed to have a firm, solid foundation for them both to stand on.

Once Mia was ready, both with her appearance and mind-set, she headed to the main house where she would work just as she did any other day.

Should she mention the pregnancy?

From a boss/employee standpoint, absolutely. But this was Bronson's mother, which forced the situation into personal territory. She honestly didn't know how to handle this delicate matter.

She and Bronson needed to have an adult conversation that didn't involve accusations and other harmful words in order to head in the right direction for this baby.

A wave of giddiness overwhelmed her as she followed the wide, palm-lined sidewalk to the patio doors of Olivia's office. For once in her life, Mia had someone to focus on other than herself. The thought both thrilled and terrified her. She didn't have the best examples of parenting growing up and she'd never been around babies, but she knew, without a doubt, that this baby would never, ever wonder if it was loved.

Love. Isn't that all anybody ever wanted? To be loved, unconditionally, just for who they are and not for their accomplishments or what they could give in return.

One day, Mia vowed, she would find that love.

"Ah, there's my beautiful assistant." Olivia poured herself a small glass of juice from the tray the cook provided every morning with fresh juices and fruit. "Care for something?"

Mia shook her head. Thanks to the crackers by her bed, she'd been able to make it here. No way was she going to jinx her good luck with anything else.

"I'm fine right now. Thanks."

Mia started to leave the office and head to her own when Olivia stopped her. "Is something wrong, dear?"

Cringing at the guilt that consumed her, Mia smiled. "Didn't sleep well last night. I'll perk up in a bit."

With a smile on her nearly wrinkle-free face, Olivia nodded. "As long as you're feeling better. Did you just have a twenty-four-hour bug?"

More like the nine-month kind.

Mia shrugged, unable to think of a way not to lie, but not to reveal the truth, either. "I'm just glad I'm able to come in today. Working from home isn't the same. I feel more productive in my office here. I did manage to complete your itinerary for the next two months and we can go over it just as soon as I get my computer booted up and check for an email confirmation for one more interview."

Fleeing before she had to stay in the same room with the woman who was her baby's grandmother, Mia went straight to her spacious office overlooking the Olympic-size pool.

The more time she could spend in here, alone, the better. Once she and Bronson had a plan, then she wouldn't feel so jittery around Olivia.

Mia sat down and turned on her computer. On a sigh she glanced at the gold-framed photograph hanging above the chaise at the other end of her office. The timeless portrait had been made into posters and paintings for decades. A young, smiling Olivia with her glossy, dark, upswept hair and body-hugging gold dress as she posed with her first Oscar...which, according to the time line Mia now knew about, was almost two years after giving up Anthony in a secret, well-paid adoption.

Mia looked at this picture in a whole new light now. A hand slid around to her flat abdomen as she thought of the fear and worry Olivia must've experienced. Mia couldn't even imagine giving up a child, but she knew Olivia must've had her reasons. What had changed in Olivia's life from that adoption to four years later when she'd given birth to Bronson?

All Mia knew was Bronson and Victoria's father had been Olivia's one and only husband. Perhaps her career and relationship status combined, forced her into giving up Anthony.

Mia couldn't help but wonder how Olivia had felt the second time she gave birth to a son. Having Bronson probably brought bittersweet memories.

Mia's thoughts always drifted back to Bronson and that night in Cannes when he'd entered her suite. She should've told him no, considering what she knew regarding Anthony, but how could she when his mouth had taken over and his hands had started their journey up her dress?

Sometimes she thought of that night and it moved through her mind in a haze of slow motion, almost as if it was a dream. Making love all night. The soft, heated whispers in the dark. The kisses. Ah, the kisses had rendered her speechless. The man had captivated her.

They had an amazing night of sex with no promises and in the final days of the festival, they'd appeared together for the cameras. Simple, no complications.

And now she was pregnant. So much for keeping it simple.

She wished more than anything that she could keep her personal feelings out of this, but she couldn't. Even though Bronson had said some hurtful things to her, she was still every bit as attracted to him as she'd been in Cannes. Perhaps if she could get that night out of her head, she'd be better off.

Except that's all that consumed her thoughts. Her days, her nights. Bronson Dane and his smooth touches, his Prince Charming–like qualities.

"Mia, darling."

Olivia's buttery-smooth voice drifting from across the grand mahogany desk pulled her from the memories of Cannes back to the fact that her lover's mother stood across from her.

"You've been staring at the screen for two minutes, and I said your name twice." Olivia smiled, crossed her arms over her ivory pants suit and tilted her head. "Would you like to talk about whatever it is that has your mind elsewhere?"

Mia closed her eyes, wishing Bronson would stay out of her head so she could work. "I'm sorry, Olivia."

The Grand Dane slid off her diamond-studded reading glasses and smiled. "My dear, you have nothing to be sorry about. Now, let's talk. What's bothering you, darling?"

Mia sighed, acknowledging that this woman was relentless in getting what she wanted. She'd given birth to three very successful children, raised two and didn't get to the top of her game by not reading other people.

Mia could talk about some things, but not the main thing.

How did she start?

"You think I don't recognize the signs?"

Mia froze. "Olivia—"

The starlet smiled. "I know when a woman is infatuated with a man. Especially when that man is my son."

Mia breathed a sigh of relief and came to her feet. "I'm not infatuated with Bronson. I'm just…" Having his baby.

"Mia, honey, I know you don't have people in your life. I know you grew up under extreme circumstances, which makes me all the more proud of how you've excelled." Olivia rested her hands, palms down, on the glossy desktop. "I was young once and I know all about matters of the heart. So, believe me when I say I've been where you are."

If only she knew how true that statement was.

Olivia had been where Mia was now. Pregnant, unwed, in a very promising career. God, how Mia wished this weren't Bronson's mother. She'd love nothing more than to confide in Olivia, to seek advice from someone who'd been in her shoes.

Mia went to the floor-to-ceiling windows and blew out a breath as she looked down to the lavish gardens and pool below. "And where am I?"

The question had been turning over and over in her mind since her world came to a crashing halt Saturday morning in her doctor's office.

"Only you can answer that," Olivia said, coming to stand beside her. "And if you can't, perhaps you should be talking to Bronson so you can get your mind back on work."

Okay, hard to take advice from a woman who didn't know all the facts. But she was right. Mia did need to talk to Bronson again. Why hadn't he called? Was he still convinced this baby wasn't his? Wouldn't he feel like an ass when he discovered she'd been telling the truth?

A gentle arm wrapped around Mia's shoulders, reminding her of how much she missed having her own mother in her life. "My darling, I can tell when another woman is at war within herself. I just want you to find some peace. And feel free to talk to me, not as your employer, not as Bronson's mother, but as a friend."

Mia looked back at their reflection in the window as tears pricked her eyes. Stupid hormones. As if the thought of having a loving family of her own weren't always on her mind, now she was coming to love the Danes a little too much. They were all seeping into her heart and she feared—no, she knew—she would end up hurt.

"I do think of you as a friend, Olivia." Mia turned, smiling at her baby's grandmother. "I have so few and I appreciate your taking time to give me advice."

"Anytime, my love." Olivia's smile was replaced by a scowl. "Now, have you told Bronson how you feel? Men can be so dense at times."

How she felt? Oh, no, this was not a conversation she was going to have. Honestly, Mia wasn't entirely sure. She certainly had some kind of feelings for Bronson, but beyond that, she couldn't say. Right now, whatever feelings she may or may not have weren't the issue. This baby had to be first and foremost on her mind.

Before she could answer, a wave of nausea overwhelmed her. Mia swayed, holding a hand up to the glass to steady herself, but Olivia took hold of her hands.

"Mia?"

"I'm okay," she assured Olivia. "I just got dizzy or something."

She closed her eyes, willing the moment to pass. Deep breath in. Deep breath out.

"Why don't you sit down." Olivia guided her to the leather desk chair. "You got awfully pale all of a sudden."

Mia took a seat, thankful the room had stopped spinning. "Really, Olivia, I'm fine."

Fine. Well, as fine as she could be, considering that the father of her baby had accused her of being a liar and having an affair with his illegitimate brother.

"Doing better now that you're sitting down?"

As if getting off her feet would make her condition better.

"Yes," Mia offered with a smile. "I'm sure I just need some juice or something. Why don't we go back to your office and I'll see what the cook put on the tray?"

"Perfect." Olivia stepped back, allowing Mia to get to her feet. "You snack and get your strength back up so we can chat about why you're hiding a pregnancy from me."

Mia's eyes darted to Olivia's steely blue ones. "Olivia, I…" She wanted to lie, she really did, but she couldn't. "I'm not hiding it. Honestly, I just found out myself."

Olivia reached out and squeezed her hands. "I'm not going to pry, because I know this is a scary time, but please know that you can come to me and discuss anything. I want to be here for you."

Mia couldn't help the tears that sprang up like a leaky faucet. "Oh, Olivia, you don't know how much I need someone to talk to."

Olivia opened her arms and Mia sank into the woman's embrace. How many times had she needed this—the love of an understanding woman? Just one hug shot straight to Mia's heart.

"I assume the baby belongs to my son." Olivia pulled back, meeting her eyes. "I saw how the two of you looked at each other in Cannes. The sparks practically singed everyone around you. Does he know?"

Mia nodded. "He does. We haven't really had a chance to talk rationally. We're both letting this sink in. And considering those rumors about me and Anthony, I'm not sure where I stand with Bronson."

"Come to my office." Olivia wrapped an arm around her shoulder and led her toward the hall. "You have a lot you need to get off your chest."

Oh, she had no idea. But at least the pregnancy was out in the open. Too bad the forty-year-old baby secret was still locked up tight. Mia had a bad feeling that Olivia would push for something between her and Bronson. But Mia refused to be in a relationship out of obligation or pity. And no way would she be with Bronson just because he or anyone else said so.

Call her naive, but she was waiting for love. She would find love, and that man would accept Mia and her baby.

Seven

When Bronson had returned from his lunch meeting with his attorney—just to discuss his options if he was indeed the father of the baby—his assistant had informed him he had a call from Mia Spinelli, stating that he had to be at her place by six o'clock. No exceptions.

Another urgent message, this time from his mother, said she needed to see him tonight, as well. Again, no exceptions. Since when did he allow his life to be controlled by demanding women?

Obviously, the baby secret was no longer a secret. He was not ready to discuss this with his mother, not until he knew all the facts and where he stood.

Bronson had barely dropped his hand after knocking when the door to the cottage swung open. There stood Mia wearing another one of those simple little strapless cotton dresses. No matter that she looked amazing, he was certainly not in the mood. And considering the current circumstances, he'd better learn to control his hormones around this woman because he would not be forced deeper into her devious plan.

"Telling my mother about the baby is your new tactic?" he asked, barging past her into the house.

Mia spun around to face him, sending the door slamming behind her. "Did she tell you that?"

So, she really had told his mother. He was just guessing by the urgency of the phone calls. Dammit, he wasn't ready for anyone to know, especially considering the last baby debacle.

"Actually, I haven't talked to her. She called my office and demanded I come to the house tonight. I'm assuming that means she knows, and I sure as hell didn't tell her."

Bronson kept his hands on his hips, ready for another fight. This was his life, his reputation. There was no backing down, no letting Mia have the upper hand. And now more than ever he needed to keep his sights on her. No way would he allow her to destroy his family...or whatever the hell else her intentions were.

"Look, I didn't call you here to argue." Mia moved past him and led him through the thick white columns separating the foyer from the living area. "We need to sit down and discuss, like adults, what we're going to do and what part you want to take in the life of our baby."

Bronson remained standing when Mia took a seat in the wing-back chair. "Let me set a few things straight, Mia. My mother's last assistant extorted nearly a million dollars from her before she was caught and imprisoned. And two years ago my ex-fiancée betrayed my trust. So you're sorely mistaken if you think, even for a second, that I'm just going to believe you when you say the baby is mine. Scandal is nothing new in Hollywood, so don't think you're going to get away with the most popular form of entrapment known."

Mia crossed those long, tanned legs. "If you're finished, I'd like to say something, too."

Bronson shoved his hands in his pockets and nodded, testing his willpower by keeping his eyes off those legs. "Fine."

"My parents were killed when I was five. After several foster homes, I realized that the only way I would ever have a family was to grow up and have one of my own."

Mia turned her head, but not before he saw the moisture gather in her eyes. He waited for her to turn back, fully engaged in a crying session in an attempt to gain his sympathy. But when she looked back up, the tears were still there, only unshed and Mia tilted her chin just a bit as if defying them. Damn, he didn't want to respect her strength.

"Family means everything, Bronson," she went on, her voice thick with emotion. "I've always dreamed of finding the perfect man for me. We'd settle down in a nice house, we'd create babies out of love and grow old together. I assure you, this scenario was not my dream. You can believe me, or you can choose to believe that I'm just as conniving as other women you've grouped me with. That's up to you. I want this baby to know its father, and I'd hate for you to miss out on the life of your child simply because you're afraid and this deceitful town has made you cynical."

Bronson turned toward the wall of windows and wished like hell she was telling the truth—and that she hadn't pegged him so easily. She wasn't the only one who'd had the idea of a family. He'd come from a loving home, one of the few the industry hadn't tainted. He'd love to someday fill his spacious home with a woman he loved and their babies. So, yeah, Mia wasn't the only one with dreams.

But his work had always come first, something his ex-fiancée had thrown in his face. And since then, he *had* turned cynical—disturbing how Mia homed in on that aspect.

"I totally understand your reasons for not believing me," she went on as he continued to stare out the window. "I can only hope my actions back up the truth. I won't ask for a dime from you, Bronson, or your family. I will continue to work for your mother and support the baby. This baby's needs have to come before your feelings."

She was right. Whether the baby was his or not, the baby didn't ask to be born, and Mia's baby had to have top priority.

So, for now, until he had medical proof, he'd assume what she said was the truth and keep a close watch on her. Because if this baby was his, there was no way in hell Mia was going to raise this child on her own.

"How are you feeling?" he asked, surprised that he really cared when, for all he knew, she was a first-rate scam artist.

A soft smile spread across her lips. "Better once lunch passes. I've been reading online, and mine is a typical pregnancy. This is all so new to me because I've never been around babies. I just can't devour enough information."

Bronson swallowed the lump of emotion. Hearing her excitement made him feel like a jerk, but he had to be cautious. His heart couldn't take another beating...or another baby ripped from his life.

"The baby is only the size of a pea right now," she added, her hand moving to her flat stomach. "Strange how something so tiny can throw off my whole system."

"I found a doctor I'd like you to start seeing. She's the best, and she will keep things quiet if this baby turns out to be mine. I don't want the press hounding you."

Mia's hand froze on her stomach, and her eyes turned to slits. "I don't want your doctor, Bronson. I have a doctor I'm quite pleased with and, I assure you, the office won't reveal who the baby's father is because I haven't said a word. Besides, it's not as if the office will ever know it's you anyway."

Bronson closed the space between them and took a seat next to her on the sofa. "I'm going to your doctor's appointments, Mia. While I'm not totally convinced this baby is mine, on the chance that it is, I want to be around for every appointment and the birth."

For a minute, Mia simply stared. Her natural beauty left him breathless—so flawless, so timeless. The camera would love her. The camera *had* loved her. He had tabloids with snapshots from Cannes to prove it.

"I will not have you believe the worst of me and expect me to let you control and watch over my pregnancy," she told him through gritted teeth. "You can either act like a father or stay away. You can't have it both ways, Bronson."

Oh, he could and he would. But she'd learn that in time. No need to argue right now.

"Fine," he agreed. "You stick with your doctor, but I'm coming to all the visits and I will ask questions if I see fit. I will also have my assistant call to make sure your appointments are kept quiet and we get right in. We shouldn't be seen in the waiting area."

Mia rolled her eyes. "They have private waiting areas, Bronson. No need to get all guard dog on me. Besides, you need to talk to your mother and sister. We can't prolong the inevitable. The media is going to find out soon anyway when I start showing."

Bronson could just imagine Mia with a rounded stomach, carrying a baby—possibly his baby. She'd be just as stunning, just as breathtaking.

Dammit, he hated being torn like this. How could he want something he'd never even had? Granted, he'd more than gotten used to the idea of being a father when his ex-fiancée was pregnant. But when she'd lost the baby, and the truth had come out that it hadn't even been his, Bronson had buried those crushed emotions and vowed never to be caught up in something that wasn't his again.

And here he was insisting he attend all of Mia's appointments for a baby that could very well be Anthony's—the very man his ex threw in his face as a potential candidate for being the father.

All the more reason to loathe the man and be suspicious of his ex-assistant.

"I'm going to the main house as soon as I leave here," he told her. "I left a message for Victoria to come over, so I'm hoping she'll be there, as well. Do you want to join me?"

Mia's eyes widened as she let out a soft gasp. "I'm not…I…Bronson, I'm not sure I'd be very good at this family meeting."

He hadn't really intended it as a question. "You'll come with me because if this baby is mine, you have bonded yourself to the Danes for the rest of your life." God help him being tied to this seductive woman forever.

"I'm so sick of your trying to control me," Mia told him, coming to her feet. "And quit acting like you're not sure you're the father. You know you are. Deep down, Bronson, you know. And it hurts me that you would deny this baby even for a second." She turned, heading toward the foyer. "Let's get this family meeting over with."

With a smile on his face, Bronson watched Mia storm out of her cottage. If his life weren't in such chaos at the moment, he'd admire her take-charge attitude and independent stance. But since his family was on the line, he needed to focus.

No way was he letting this temptress under his skin again. From now on he'd be on guard and ready for whatever she threw his way.

Dread, excitement, fear and anxiety all rolled into one big ball of nerves and settled deep into Mia's stomach as she and Bronson entered the main house.

Olivia stood in the formal living room next to the wall of shelves that housed many pictures from her early days in movies as well as several professional pictures of Victoria and Bronson as children. Most of the photos were personal, showcasing the movie family in real life. Swimming in the pool as children, Victoria as a teen ballerina, a young Bronson on the shoulders of his father.

Mia pulled herself out of the Dane family snapshots and into reality. One day maybe her child would be in a frame in this very room. Mia hoped so. That was one of the things she'd missed as an adult. There were very few pictures of her as a child, though she still had the two photos of her and her parents when they'd first come to America. Those captured moments were something she treasured every day.

She slid a hand over her locket, reminding herself that she was never alone in life's endeavors, even if she felt that way at times.

Soft laughter pulled Mia from her thoughts. Victoria sat in the white club chair on her cell phone speaking French and laughing at someone named Jacques. But once Mia and Bronson fully entered the room, Olivia's face softened with a genuine smile and Victoria ended her call.

"I'm assuming Mother told you the news about the baby." Bronson eyed Victoria who simply nodded. "I just want to get this all out so there's no confusion as to where I stand and what's going on."

Mia wanted to throw up. Undoubtedly Bronson would

start the same song and dance she'd heard the past two days about "if" the baby was his. No matter how harsh those words sounded and how she hated him for saying them, she knew he was just as scared as she was.

"I will assume this baby is mine for now," he went on. "But we will get a DNA test to determine the father."

"I never agreed to that," she piped in. "You assumed I would, but since I don't want your money, it's a moot point."

Bronson turned on her. "You will have a DNA test done on the child, Mia. Forget yourself for a minute, will you? If this child is a Dane, he has a sizable fortune he's set to inherit."

"Are you kidding me?"

Mia glanced around to Victoria who was now on her feet, hands on her hips. "You're acting like this is a business arrangement. You're talking about a child for crying out loud, Bron. *Your* child. You may have been caught off guard the last time, but I believe Mia. She wouldn't lie about the paternity."

A bit of elation spread through Mia at Victoria's confidence that she wasn't trying to swindle anything from this family, especially since they'd only known her about seven months. But what did she mean about "last time"?

"You just want the baby to be mine," Bronson said. "Don't start sewing designer Onesies."

"You want the baby, too." Olivia moved toward them. "There's no need to deny it, Bronson. I know you're scared to death to admit this is your child for fear of losing another baby. But I agree with Victoria. Mia isn't lying. I've gotten to know her very well, and this is an honest, loyal woman."

She wasn't feeling so loyal at the moment, considering the secret she held. Oh, she was being honest about *this* baby, but not so much about the baby Olivia gave up nearly forty years ago.

Talk about intense. This was why Mia didn't want to do family meetings. First of all, she wasn't in the family and, second of all, old wounds always reopened and Mia certainly didn't want to add that dash of salt into Bronson's.

But what was all this talk of the baby he lost? They made it sound as if that baby wasn't his. But surely if his ex-fiancée was pregnant, the baby had been his. Hadn't it? Good Lord, was there another buried Dane scandal? What kind of mess had she stepped into?

"I'm not here to discuss my past," Bronson declared, eyeing his mother and sister. "I'm here to let you all know that this baby is between me and Mia for the time being. I don't want you two fawning all over her and getting attached to someone who may not even belong in this family."

"Excuse me," Mia chimed in. "This baby is as much a Dane as it is a Spinelli. If your mother and sister want to get *attached,* let them. Just because you are choosing to keep your distance doesn't mean they have to. My whole life I wanted to be part of a family." Mia clutched her locket and choked back tears. "My whole *life.* Do you know what that's like?"

Mia stared at Bronson, not caring a bit that Olivia and Victoria were listening, not caring that her voice was cracking. She was standing up for her child, as no one had done for her after her parents' death, and she was starting now. This child would know love and security from day one.

"I never really felt a sense of belonging. Once my parents were killed…" She hesitated, praying the tears stinging her eyes wouldn't spill over. "I will not have our child wondering where he or she belongs. I want nothing but love for this child. You can keep every last dollar. Just don't deny the fact this child does belong here just as much as you do. Don't deny our baby the bond only a loving family can provide."

Mia caught sight of Olivia and Victoria, and both women had glistening tears and soft smiles. Bronson, on the other hand, still wore the signature scowl he'd had in place since he'd learned the truth. What would it take to get him to look on the bright side? Try to make this a positive time?

"I'm sure you all need to talk, so I'll let you have your privacy."

Mia turned on her heel and left the room. She didn't slow down until she was far enough away from the house that no one would see her break into tears.

She'd never been much of a crier. Life had toughened her up at a young age, but lately she couldn't stop the tears. Whether it was the uncontrollable hormones or the fact that she just didn't want her baby to feel neglected and abandoned, she didn't know. What she did know is that it was quite obvious the Dane women were perfectly comfortable with the idea that this baby belonged in the family. Too bad Bronson believed the worst.

And that's what hurt the most. Had he always believed the worst in her? When he'd slept with her, had he just been passing time?

Mia hated the thought that she'd slept with Bronson out of pure lust. She'd never slept with a man only because she found him attractive. But it wasn't just that Bronson was curl-your-toes sexy. He had been so smooth, so seductive, and with the ambiance of Cannes and all the romance surrounding them, she'd been caught up in a whirlwind. But she'd be damned if she let her lack of good judgment affect her child's life or what Bronson thought of her.

This baby would have everything she never did: stability, unconditional love and family. Mia would settle for nothing less.

Eight

The next month flew by without any major drama—baby or otherwise. Anthony still hadn't confronted Olivia, and Bronson was still as personable as a bedsheet when he'd call twice daily to ask how she was feeling.

But today was the day of her first prenatal visit, and Bronson would be picking her up any minute.

This should be a fun ride.

As if the strained phone conversations weren't enough, now she had to sit in close proximity to the man she found both insufferable and devastatingly attractive at the same time. She couldn't blame any of this on her hormones. Bronson was still just as sexy, and every time she looked at him she couldn't help but remember their night together.

She so wished she could forget how amazing his hands felt as they'd glided over her body. The way he held her, giving so much of himself. Mia had never before experienced anything like it, and she had a feeling she never would again. Yes, the sex had been hurried, frantic, but Bronson had been so in tune with her body, so perfect for her.

When Mia's doorbell rang, she grabbed her purse and keys and opened the door to a still-sexy Bronson. She reset the alarm and closed the door behind her. Without a word, Bronson led her to his two-door sports car. At least he had the decency to open the passenger door for her.

"This'll be a blast," she muttered to the empty car as he walked around the hood.

As soon as he got in and brought the engine to life, Mia twisted in her seat. "You don't have to go. No one will think anything if you just stay away. I've already given you the out you obviously want. I expect nothing from you."

Bronson's grip tightened on the wheel, the muscle ticking in his jaw. "I said I'd be there for every appointment in case the baby is mine. I meant it. My assistant has already called to ensure we will be taken back immediately."

Mia wasn't going to argue. In truth, she wanted to share this glorious time with someone, she just wished that someone shared her excitement.

And she was excited—more and more every day. The baby was coming whether she'd planned for it or not. True, the fear still overwhelmed her at times, but in all honesty, she was happy about this little person growing inside her. She'd even had a burst of giddiness this morning when her skirt had been snug.

"You're happy?"

Mia glanced back over to Bronson. "Excuse me?"

He threw her a glance. "You were smiling. You're happy about this."

"The baby, yes. The situation, not really." She smoothed her short cotton skirt over her knees. "I won't lie. The more I think about this baby, the more excited I get. But I do wish I was at a different place in my life. I've always envisioned myself married before having kids."

He said nothing, and Mia wasn't sure she even wanted to know what he thought. Other than her giving him directions to the doctor's office, nothing else was discussed. Obviously, he didn't want things to get too personal, and that was fine with her. If he was going to be a jerk about this, she didn't want to open up her feelings to him. He didn't deserve to be privy to her thoughts.

Once they were in the office, Bronson's tension meter skyrocketed as his shoulders stiffened and his gaze moved around the room. They were immediately shown to a private waiting area, complete with a closed door. Considering Hollywood's lame attempt to keep things hush-hush, Mia assumed every doctor's office had private waiting areas like this one.

"You okay?" she whispered as she filled out all the documents about her medical history.

"Fine."

Mia let it go and proceeded with the questions. She knew her information, but when it came to the father, she was a bit uncomfortable asking.

"Could you um…" She nudged the clipboard and paper onto his lap and handed him the pen. "I need you to fill this section out."

His eyes darted down, then back up to her. "Can't you leave it blank?"

"If I didn't know who the father was I would. But since you're here, fill it out and pretend this isn't torturous."

She'd seriously had it with his take on the pregnancy. He didn't want to acknowledge the baby was his because he was scared of losing another one. But the least he could do was be supportive of her. Not financially, but some conversation or even a smile now and then would help.

Lord have mercy, would he ever believe that she wasn't out to sabotage his family? She could only hope time and her actions would prove her innocence.

He grabbed the pen, began reading then checking the appropriate boxes next to family history of illnesses and diseases. Mia stared at the paper, jealous that he actually had a family history that he knew about, had heard stories about. That is what she wanted for her child. That sense of family, a unit.

Mia had only been able to answer the questions strictly on what she had been told about her birth parents. Beyond them, she knew nothing about her family back in Italy. Her mother had been a diabetic, but other than that, she didn't know about any major health issues.

Tracing a finger over the scar on her hand, Mia silently vowed to her unborn baby that there would always be stability, always a place to call home.

"Here." Bronson handed the clipboard back to her. "I'm done."

She took the forms out to the receptionist and within minutes they were called back to the exam room. When the nurse told Mia to change into the gown, her eyes darted to Bronson. He merely lifted a brow as the nurse left the room.

"I'll just change in here." She motioned to the bathroom.

As Mia put on the paper-thin gown, she nearly laughed at how modesty now overtook her. The man had touched, tasted and savored every inch of her body. And he would probably be in the delivery room.

Yeah, modesty definitely had no place here. Her needs were no longer a priority. Her baby trumped everything and everyone.

Mia put on the hospital footies and padded back out to the exam table, holding her gown together with a fisted hand. Bronson's presence filled the room as he sat in the corner in a plastic chair.

"What will they do today?" he asked.

Mia's heart softened a little. She knew he was nervous. He'd lost a baby once before. He may have his doubts about whether or not he was the father, but she could tell he was getting more used to the idea.

"I think they listen for a heartbeat and maybe do an ultrasound to see exactly how far along I am."

"I came to a couple appointments the first time…" He trailed off, looking her in the eye. "Never mind. Let's just focus on now."

Mia wanted to say something, to not let this intimate moment pass her by. For a split second he'd thought of opening up to her, and she realized she wanted that more than she'd thought. She did want a connection to Bronson, other than a physical one, if for no other reason than for the sake of the baby. Could they work backward and attempt at least a friendship? Would he ever feel comfortable enough to not close up when personal issues arose?

The door swung open and Mia smiled at her doctor.

"Good afternoon, Mia," Dr. Bender said. "How are you feeling today?"

Mia nodded. "I'm adjusting to the morning sickness and I know to keep food by my bed and eat before I even think about standing up."

The doctor washed and dried her hands at the sink in the corner. "You should be nearing the end of the queasiness. Not many women have morning sickness through their entire pregnancy."

The entire pregnancy? Mia couldn't even fathom that. She prayed she had the typical first trimester kind and the sickness would end soon.

Dr. Bender moved around the exam table. "Just lie back

here and let's listen for the heartbeat." She eased Mia down and glanced over to Bronson. "You're the father?"

Mia didn't look at him, didn't want to see his denial, but she was even more crushed when he spoke.

"How soon can a DNA test be done?" he asked.

The doctor placed a sheet over Mia's legs, then folded the gown up to expose her belly and squirted some cool gel onto her stomach. She began to move the Doppler around, spreading the sticky gel, obviously not fazed by Bronson's question.

Mia, on the other hand, wanted to cry. How dare he humiliate her like this? Even worse, how could he deny this baby in public? Besides making it sound as if she slept around, he was disrespecting their child.

"That depends," Dr. Bender said. "There is one test called chorionic villus sampling, which can be done between ten and fourteen weeks. The other is called an amniocentesis, which is done between fourteen and twenty weeks. I can go over the procedures and the risks involved if you'd like before you make a decision."

Amid all the static of the Doppler machine and the doctor telling Bronson about the testing, Mia heard it. The rapid thump, thump, thump of her baby's heartbeat.

Her baby. Her eyes darted to Bronson. Their baby.

"Baby's heart rate is right at the norm for eleven weeks." The doctor wiped off the gel from Mia's stomach. "Sounds like you've got a healthy one. Are you experiencing any other symptoms, other than morning sickness?"

"Just some slight cramping," Mia told her. "I get dizzy sometimes."

"You never told me that," Bronson piped up, suddenly more concerned.

Eyes wide, Mia threw him a look. Now was certainly not the time to discuss why she hadn't told him—because he'd barely given her two minutes when he'd called on the phone. Besides, if he'd acted halfway as if he genuinely cared, she would have made the time to open up to him.

"That's fairly normal," the doctor told her, taking a seat on her black stool. "Your uterus is stretching, so that will cause some cramping. Try to rest as much as possible. If a miscarriage happens, it's more than likely going to happen within the first twelve weeks from conception. I don't say that to scare you. I just want you to listen to your body and take good care of yourself."

"I'll see that she does."

Mia fisted her hands at her side. Now he chose to step up? Now he wanted to offer to help? And what did he mean by *he'd see that she takes care of herself?* Did he plan on spending more time with her?

When the rest of the exam was done and she got herself dressed, Mia scheduled an ultrasound for next month and didn't wait for Bronson before she made quick steps back to his car.

She wasn't sure what she was most angry at. His abrupt questioning about the DNA, that he acted like he cared once she'd mentioned her symptoms or that he had the doctor laughing at his witty charm by the end of the appointment.

Damn that man. She just wanted to throttle him for making her so aware that her feelings weren't slacking at all…if anything they were growing stronger.

The man oozed sex appeal, he charmed everyone he came in contact with and he'd starred in nearly all her dreams since they'd left Cannes. One would think, in light of the situation, she'd learned her lesson not to fall for the charm, but unfortunately her mind and her heart were not receiving the same memo.

So now she wasn't only angry with him for his accusations and attitude toward her, she was furious with herself for getting all tied up in knots over a man she'd let work his way into her life. Permanently.

By the time Bronson pulled in front of Mia's cottage, he knew he was not going to get an invite inside. He also knew that wouldn't stop him.

He opened her car door, took her hand to help her out and kept holding it, even when she tugged. He wasn't letting her off the hook that easily.

She'd driven him crazy from the second she'd stepped out of her house. Immediately he'd noticed the change in her body from her fuller breasts to her thicker waist. She'd looked completely simple in layered colorful tanks that hugged her slightly rounded belly and a plain cotton skirt, showcasing those killer legs. Her ensemble was utterly sexy.

Added to that, her protectiveness of the baby, her adamant stance that she wanted a stable life for her child—maybe his child—was just another aspect that made her even more attractive.

Everything about her was sexy, and Bronson wished like hell he could get those thoughts out of his mind.

But how could he when she was very likely carrying his child? How could he deny that he still wanted this woman, whether she was lying or not? And how the hell had he let his emotions slip from his grasp? He seriously had no control as far as Mia was concerned, and that could prove to be catastrophic.

Every time he thought of the baby, he thought back to Cannes, when he'd wanted her and nothing else mattered. He always got what he wanted; there were never consequences. Until now.

Mia unlocked her door and reached in to type in her security code. "Thank you for taking me," she told him, obviously trying to block him from coming in. "I have a lot of work to catch up on after taking a few hours off."

Bronson knew his mother cared more about this baby, which could be a Dane heir, than whatever work she'd put on Mia's schedule.

"I'm coming in."

She eyed him and he waited for the argument. Surprised when she moved from the door, Bronson followed her in.

"In case you missed my not-so-subtle silent treatment, I'm not in the best of moods right now," she told him, heading to the kitchen. "I cannot believe you asked the doctor about a DNA test. I just can't…"

Because she really didn't want him to uncover the truth or had that question really upset her?

Mia had made this kitchen her own with an array of cooking magazines spread open on the counter next to the stove. A very impressive spice rack sat next to an even more impressive knife set.

"You know it has to be done, Mia." He watched as she reached for a handful of M&M's from a glass candy dish on the center island. "The sooner we know, the sooner plans can be made."

She laid out an assortment of colors, moving the green ones to the side. "I do know, Bronson. I know you're the father. I don't care about having a test after the baby is born, if it will ease your mind, but I will not put this baby in jeopardy right now just to satisfy you. The doctor went over the risks. I'm not willing to chance a miscarriage or harm this baby in any way."

"Then we'll have the test as soon as the baby's born," he told her, watching her pick through her candy like a child. "No excuses then."

Intrigued, he watched as she ate all the other colors, but saved the green ones for last. "You don't like green?"

She eyed the candy, then looked up to him. "They're my favorite. I always save the best for last."

He watched her dainty, pink-polished fingertips pick up one green piece at a time and pop it into her mouth. Why did he have this urge to feed them to her? She could very well be playing him. But damn if he wasn't starting to have doubts about that. Emotionally, he couldn't afford to go down this path again.

He tried not to think of her phoning Anthony to discuss how quickly and easily she'd gotten so personal with Bronson's family. But he couldn't dismiss the reality that she could be doing just that. So many emotions—both for and against Mia—and he didn't know where to place them all. Unfortunately, they'd conglomerated into one large ball of anger and frustration. What he needed to do was stay focused on work...the one aspect of his life he had control over lately.

He'd met with his mother this week, and they'd finalized the movie script and budget. Now he had to put the wheels in motion to produce it, and then they could make the grand announcement. The media had their ideas about the secret project he was working on, considering he'd been so private about it, but they hadn't guessed yet.

And he intended for no one to find out until he and his mother were ready. That included the stunning woman standing across from him, possibly carrying his child. His mother had really done some work to keep this project a secret from Mia.

"You're awfully quiet for someone who came in uninvited." She spoke without looking up as she pulled out another handful of candy and proceeded to separate them. "Something on your mind?"

The fact that he still wanted her just as badly as he had in Cannes. Liar or not, this woman turned him on by simply standing there. Hadn't he learned his lesson after the last deceitful beauty?

Bronson knew he needed to keep a closer eye on Mia. If she were out to destroy him, he'd break her. And if not, well, they could at least have some fun along the way.

But that seed of doubt had been planted in his mind once he saw how genuine she was regarding this child. Was she telling the truth? Had this pregnancy been unplanned and was he indeed the father?

Common sense told him no, but his heart was starting to get involved as far as this child was concerned, and he wanted so much to believe her.

Taking a seat at the wrought-iron barstool, he reached for one of her precious green M&M's. "I actually thought we should spend some time together. You are so adamant this baby's mine, so I'd like to know what you expect from me. You've stressed it's not money. What is it?"

Mia's hand froze as she reached for another green piece. "I don't want anything from you, Bronson. Not for me anyway. I want this baby to have a loving father. That's all."

She met his eyes on those final words, and the sincerity he saw nearly put a choke hold on him. Either he was becoming a pushover or she was telling the truth. Time would tell.

"I promise, if this baby is indeed mine, he will know no stronger or deeper love."

That was something Bronson didn't have to think about. This baby would be a Dane and have everything at his disposal. He'd never lack for stability or love.

"What about for yourself, Mia?" Bronson stood, came

around the bar and leaned against the counter right next to her. "What do you want?"

Her hand trembled as she placed the glass lid back on the candy dish. "Nothing. I already told you."

She was crumbling. Now he just had to push a little harder. If she were lying, he'd discover it, and God help her if he didn't like what he found.

With his index finger, he grazed her cheek, her chin, until she turned to look at him. "If this baby's mine, there can't be any lies between us. Starting now. What do you want, Mia?"

"Nothing." Her eyes betrayed her as they darted down to his mouth and back up. "There's nothing I…need."

That statement alone just proved she was a liar. And he didn't know if he was pushing her to torment her or himself, but he had a feeling they were both equally uncomfortable right now.

Which was all the more reason for him to take charge.

Bronson couldn't stop his lips from claiming hers any more than he could stop the arousal that punched him whenever he so much as thought of her.

He hadn't gotten to where he was in life by riding on the coattails of his name. Nor had he gotten there by being weak.

But Mia was working her way into his life, causing a weakness he couldn't afford.

Literally.

Nine

Mia had wanted to feel those lips on hers again but never thought she would. So she'd lied when she said she didn't want anything. She couldn't very well tell Bronson she wanted him again, could she? He was so skeptical of her, and if she wanted that family she'd dreamed of, she'd have to take it slow and make him see she was the real deal.

As Bronson's hands slid up to cup the sides of her face, Mia realized that's exactly what she wanted. She wanted to see where this attraction would lead. He couldn't very well deny that he was physically attracted to her…she could feel the evidence.

Mia wrapped her arms around his neck and gave in to the kiss as Bronson changed the angle. She arched her back, pressing her sensitive breasts against his solid chest.

What had happened to make him turn from being so irritated at her to devouring her in her kitchen?

Mia eased back. "What was that for?"

Dark eyes filled with desire stared back at her. "You may not need anything, Mia, but I do. I've tried to keep my hands off you. I've tried to keep my distance because I didn't want to complicate anything with this pregnancy, but I can't."

Really? Was this a game or was he sincere?

"But you don't believe me."

Bronson rested his forehead against hers and sighed. "I want to, God do I want to. I want this baby to be a Dane."

Mia's heart clenched at the battle he waged within himself. And he'd admitted his fears aloud—that shocked her. His frustrated tone and moment of vulnerability revealed more about his state of mind than he'd probably intended.

She reached up, grasping his biceps. "Then let yourself believe and I swear to you, you won't get hurt."

At least not about this. About Anthony being his biological brother...that wasn't her secret to tell, and she could only pray her loyalty and vow of silence didn't blow up in her face.

Bronson stepped back, shoving his hands in his pockets. The muscle ticked in his jaw as he glanced out the French doors to the hot-tub area. "All I can offer is a physical relationship, Mia. I have nothing else to give a woman at this stage in my life. I promise if this child's mine, I'll love it beyond measure. But if you're under the impression that you and I can forge a relationship—much less a marriage—we can't."

She hadn't been under that impression. Of course, that didn't stop her from hoping and dreaming for a family of her own. But she wouldn't push—that's not how she wanted to obtain her family. She would hold out for love.

So while spending more time with Bronson might exact a toll on her emotionally, she was willing to take the chance because she believed there was so much more than physicality to explore between them.

"I just want us to get along for the sake of the baby," she told him. "If anything happens between us, physical or otherwise, we'll deal with that when the time comes. For right now, this baby is my main concern. Not your needs and not mine."

Bronson's eyes came back to her. "You're going to be a great mother."

Mia's throat tightened, and her belly fluttered. She was going to be a mother. What she wouldn't give to be able to go to her own for advice right now.

She could get through this on her own. She had no choice. Although she had a feeling that getting her heart involved with Bronson was going to lead to a bigger heartache than she could ever imagine.

After three weeks of life getting back to normal, Mia thanked God every day that her morning sickness didn't rear its ugly head. Nausea occasionally followed her around like an unwanted friend, but other than that, she felt fine. Bronson had called and stopped by, but nothing intimate had even come close to transpiring again, and her hormones were screaming for one more touch.

Just as Mia was turning off her computer for the day, Olivia stepped into her office. "Do you have a minute or do you need to go?" she asked.

"I'm in no hurry. I'm just going home to try a new recipe I saw in a magazine." Mia sat back down in her chair. "Something wrong?"

"Not at all. I want to commend you for how well you're handling this pregnancy, considering my son's doubts."

Mia really didn't want to get into what she and Bronson discussed. Working with the grandmother of her child while wanting Bronson more in her life could get a bit awkward.

"I'm not trying to pry," Olivia said, as if reading her thoughts. "But I do want to offer some money to help with the baby's furniture, clothes, whatever you want to buy."

Mia came to her feet. "Oh, no. I'm not taking any money, Olivia. What you pay me is more than enough, and I've been setting some aside in my savings for anything this baby may need."

"I didn't think you'd take it, but I had to offer."

"No, you didn't. I will be just fine and so will the baby, no matter what Bronson decides."

Olivia crossed her arms over her bright orange silk tunic. "Well, I don't care what my son or you say, I will be spoiling my grandchild, so you tell me when you decide on furniture or a nursery theme. I have a wonderful designer, if you're interested."

Mia laughed. "I hadn't even thought that far ahead yet."

"Oh, yes, you have."

"Okay, maybe I have," Mia conceded. "But not much. I want to find out the sex of the baby before I decide on the colors. And I'd really like to do everything myself."

Olivia shook her head. "Stubborn and independent. My son has his work cut out for him. At least say you'll hire someone to paint. You don't need to be smelling those fumes."

How could anyone not love this woman? She was so caring, so take-charge, so motherly.

"I promise."

Olivia moved around the side of the desk and came within a foot of Mia. "I have to tell you this because I'm a mother and because I love my son and have come to care about you like family. Don't let Bronson's attitude deter you if you want him in your life."

"Pardon?" Olivia wasn't really going to attempt her hand at cupid's bow, was she?

Olivia laid a gold-ringed hand on Mia's arm. "This baby has scared him more than he'll ever admit. The last time… it didn't end well. There are things you don't know, and it's his place to tell you if he chooses. I just don't want you to think everything is as it seems with him."

"I won't pry into his past, Olivia." Mia smiled, touched that this Hollywood icon valued her family more than anything else. "Right now we are getting along for the sake of the baby. What I want, what he wants, doesn't matter."

Olivia cupped Mia's cheek. "Oh, my darling, you're so wrong. You're a unit whether you like it or not. Everyone's happiness counts. Don't shove your own desires aside, especially now when you need people in your life."

Mia knew she needed people. She'd never wanted to need anyone, but she had to think realistically and see that she was out of her league here. She would need help and guidance with this child.

"I'll let you know about that painter," Mia said, hugging Olivia.

Mia left her office and walked out through Olivia's as she always did. The summer evening breeze wasn't quite so stifling tonight, and Mia lifted her face to the sky, feeling confident she was heading in the right direction with her life.

For now there was no turmoil, or not as much as there had been, and that suited Mia just fine. She hated drama—ironic since she loved working in Hollywood.

As she walked along the wide concrete path back to her house, she resisted the urge to call Anthony. She wanted to share her good news with him because they were friends, but she didn't want to add any more issues to his home life.

She also wished she could talk to him about broaching

the delicate subject with Olivia. The guilt she carried was pointless since she couldn't say anything. How she wished she could go back to that day in Anthony's office and *not* open that file he'd had on his desk. Why did she have to uncover a secret that had been buried for decades?

"Good evening."

Mia squealed, jumping back with a hand to her heart. "Bronson! You scared me to death."

If she hadn't been so lost in thought, she would've noticed him sitting on her porch looking sexy as ever. Of course, he'd show up out of the blue. That's what he did. Oh, he called every morning, but with his crazy work schedule, which changed from day to day, she never knew when he'd make a surprise visit.

"I didn't mean to scare you." He came to his feet and took her hand as she ascended the steps. "Were you lost in thought?"

Yeah, thinking about your brother.

"Something like that," she told him as she fished out her key from her bag. "How long have you been waiting?"

"Just a few minutes."

She led him inside, turned off the alarm and set her purse and keys on the foyer table. "I was just going to fix dinner. You hungry?"

A slow, cautious, sexy smile spread across his face. "Starving. I'd help, but the cook always kicked me out when I was a kid. So maybe I'll just observe."

Mia laughed as she toed off her heels and headed toward the kitchen. "I can turn on the TV if you'd like to watch something."

She moved toward the flat screen on the wall between the breakfast nook and the kitchen.

"No, I'd rather have conversation or silence. My brain is on overload right now."

Mia didn't question what was wrong. He didn't want to do personal and she could live with that…for now. But he was here, wanted to stay for dinner. Something drew him to her and she wasn't going to question it.

She pulled one of her cooking magazines from her stack beside the fridge and turned to the earmarked page. As she bustled around the kitchen pulling out ingredients and double-checking the list, she was hyperaware of his presence. He didn't say a word, but the shuffling of his rolling up the sleeves of his white dress shirt and the smell of his masculine aroma filled her kitchen.

"Feeling okay today?" he asked as she preheated the oven.

"I'm fine. I can't wait until the ultrasound." Mia pulled out a mixing bowl and stared across the island at Bronson. "I just want to see her."

"Her?" he asked, raising a brow.

Mia laughed. "I go back and forth using her or him. I don't care what we have."

Bronson's shoulders tensed.

"Sorry." Mia cringed as she turned to get a pan. "I didn't mean to make you uncomfortable."

Silence settled in once again as she mixed and poured everything into the baking stone. Once she had the dish in the oven, she wiped her hands on a towel and turned to Bronson.

"That has to bake for about an hour. Do you want some wine or a drink?"

"No, I'm good."

Mia couldn't take it another minute. She just had to uncover the truth Olivia spoke of.

"I know it's not my place to pry, but I need to know about your ex-fiancée and the baby."

Bronson's eyes turned dark as he jerked his gaze to hers. "No, you don't. There's nothing that concerns you."

Mia wet a rag and wiped off the counter. She needed a prop for her nervous hands. "Actually, it does involve me, considering you're hesitant about everything because of your past. Your ex-fiancée is always in the room with us, whether you realize it or not."

"Leave it alone, Mia."

For once she was not going to back down. "You know all about my life. You know why this baby means so much to me. I want to know why this baby scares you to the point that you can't even discuss it without tensing up."

Bronson came to his feet, running a hand through his stylishly messy hair. "I don't know why you think now is the time to rehash all this."

"I've been wondering for a while, Bronson, and today your mother—"

He jerked around. "My mother? You've got to be kidding. Did she tell you I loved that child, that his name was chosen and that I could hardly work for all the anticipation surrounding my upcoming marriage and baby?"

Mia tossed the rag into the sink. "She just said that—"

"What?" He threw his arms out to the side. "She said what? That my ex-fiancée was sleeping around behind my back and the baby wasn't mine? Oh, and did she tell you how I believed the baby belonged to Anthony?"

Breath caught in Mia's throat. Anthony the father? That couldn't be. He loved his wife more than anything and was fighting to save his marriage.

She placed her palms on the island and stared into his tormented eyes. "Oh, God, Bronson. I had no idea."

"No, but you had to push and push until I gave in. Well, congratulations. Now you know my secret." He muttered a curse. "I don't know how that wasn't leaked to the media.

They all assumed we split over her losing the baby, that the stress was too much."

Mia remembered reading that, hearing those rumors. Now she understood why this DNA test was so important... especially considering the rumors about *her* and Anthony and after he'd seen them talking in Cannes.

"That's why you don't believe me," she whispered. "All of that in your past, added to my history with Anthony, has stacked the deck against me and instantly put you on guard. In Cannes, even, you probably thought I was working for the enemy. You slept with me with all these hateful thoughts in your head. I swear, Bronson, I never even entertained thoughts of sleeping with Anthony."

Mia turned, holding a hand over her slightly rounded stomach. She didn't want any of this ugliness to touch her baby.

"Maybe dinner was a bad idea." She kept her gaze down, her body facing away from him. She couldn't look him in the eye right now. Not when she knew so much hurt was swimming in hers. "I honestly didn't meant to hurt you, to make you relive that nightmare. But I can't be around someone who believes everything I say is a lie."

Bronson's hands came up to her shoulders. "Dinner isn't a bad idea at all. I want to spend time with you, Mia. I didn't mean to yell at you. I just wanted you to see where I'm coming from."

Mia allowed those strong hands to turn her around, and she studied those eyes that showed so much emotion. It was probably a good thing he was on the other side of the camera. No way could he ever hide his true thoughts.

"I see a lot of pain," she told him, smoothing the line between his brows. "I see a man who wants to hope and is afraid to. If you'll look back at me, really look, you'll see we aren't so different."

And then she did something she'd been dying to do—
even with the accusations, the lies, the uncertainty.

Taking control of the situation, she rose on her bare toes
and kissed him.

Ten

He was toast.

Bronson knew when he'd been waiting on her porch that if she so much as hinted that she wanted physical contact, he'd be all over her. He'd been wanting her for weeks. Not just a kiss, either.

And her pressing her lips, her body, against his was much more than a hint—it couldn't get more obvious than that.

Bronson wrapped his arms around her waist and picked her up, holding her body against his. She'd read into his feelings, his emotions too well, and that scared the hell out of him. He didn't want to be under her scope—he didn't want pity.

He wanted to know if she was trying to trap and destroy him.

But most of all he wanted to know what she wore beneath her simple black skirt and sleeveless pink top.

Mia framed his face with her palms and moaned as his mouth traveled from her lips down her neck. She arched into him, sending all kinds of jolts throughout his body.

"Bronson, we—"

"Need fewer clothes."

He hated the loss of control he had as far as she was concerned. Hated that she had the power to ruin him.

But right now, Mia's breathy sighs and pants in his ear clearly overrode common sense.

"Dinner…"

He nipped at her lips. "Still has a while and I need you now."

Mia's eyes widened, then softened as a smile spread across her face. "I didn't think you liked me."

Bronson palmed her breasts through her silk top. "I like you, Mia. I still can't trust that you're telling me the whole truth, but right now, I don't give a damn."

She started to protest when his mouth settled over hers. He didn't want to hear excuses or reasons they should not be together. He knew them already and chose to ignore them.

He slid his hands around to the waist of her skirt and moved the zipper down. She wiggled those mesmerizing hips until the unwanted garment fell to the floor with a whoosh. She pulled the silk top over her head and tossed it toward the breakfast area, leaving her in a sexy, pink, lacey bra-and-panty set. Her rounded belly wasn't the only sign of pregnancy. Her breasts nearly spilled over the top of the lace.

"You destroy me," he muttered before pulling her body back against his. "Utterly destroy me."

He devoured her mouth as her hands made quick work of his belt and pants. He kicked off his shoes and stepped out of his pants, then lifted her onto the kitchen island and stepped between her legs.

"Just to be clear, I'm going to have you again tonight on a bed."

Mia smiled, tracing his lips with her fingertip. "Count on it."

He pulled her bra cups aside and slid his hands over her bare breasts, pleased when she moaned and arched into his touch. Wrapping one arm around her waist, he pulled her against the edge of the counter.

"Do we need a…" She trailed off, her eyes questioning.

"It's a little late for that," he told her. "Besides, I've always used one and I just had a routine physical. I'm clean."

"Me, too. I had complete bloodwork for my prenatal appointment."

He smiled, easing into her. "That settles it then."

Mia's arms came around his neck as her hips tilted against his. This woman was becoming a drug in his system that he couldn't get enough of. Those little moans, the sighs and the way she fit against him only proved to him how much she wanted this. She wasn't immune to their sexual chemistry.

He slid into her slowly, wanting this to last, knowing it wouldn't. He'd desired her, ached for her since Cannes. Wondered if he'd imagined how good they were together.

He hadn't. No, those dreams he'd had every night since were spot-on.

Bronson shoved aside all thoughts, focusing on the woman writhing in his arms, whispering his name. In no time she shuddered against him, sending him into his own tailspin. He held on to her until they both stopped shaking and silently vowed to make this better later in that promised bed.

As he eased back, he couldn't help but wonder how this would affect their...what? Relationship? They didn't really have a relationship. They'd supposedly made a child, but what should he call what they had?

Regardless of what this arrangement was called, he knew he wanted Mia again and he had no intention of leaving her house tonight. And the deeper he became involved with her, the more he wanted to trust every word that came out of her mouth.

Mia poured an after-dinner drink for Bronson and moved into the living room where he'd settled and was flipping through to find a movie, his gloriously tanned broad shoulders and bare chest on display for her to appreciate.

"Really?" she asked, setting his drink on the glass side table. "A movie?"

He eyed her. "We can start one, but if you try seducing me, I reserve the right to turn it off."

Was he actually going to stay? Did he want to play house? Mia was so confused by his actions because they contradicted his words. She didn't want to play games, didn't want to wait around until he decided where they stood. She just didn't have the emotional stamina for it.

"We need to talk," she told him, sitting down beside him. "I'm all for what happened before dinner, but I have to be honest—I'm not looking for a fling, Bronson. I think there could be something between us if we could just be honest with each other and not keep this so shallow."

His hand froze on the remote before he laid it down on the table. "I've told you I can't offer more to a woman, Mia. I just can't. You know why."

"I know what happened in your past," she retorted. "Let

go of it and move on. Let those wounds stay covered and stop reopening them."

He turned his head and sighed. "Mia, I'm not looking for happily-ever-after. I used to, but that's gone. Now I'm focused on work, and I have more than one project going. What I have to offer is minimal."

Meaning sex. Mia placed a hand on his arm. She knew he was softening—she'd seen it in the doctor's office when he'd heard their baby's heartbeat. She also knew their chemistry was amazing. So many elements to make for a wonderful family if he would just open his eyes to the possibility.

Patience. She had to learn patience if she wanted to forge a family with Bronson. And if the compatibility wasn't there, then she'd let it go. But she had to try. Her heart had already gotten entangled with him.

Mia started unbuttoning Bronson's dress shirt, which she'd thrown on before dinner. One by one his eyes traveled the path of her fingers.

"Then I'll take what you have to offer," she told him, shrugging out of the oversized shirt. "But I won't stop trying to make you happy and to show you how good we could be together."

She came to her feet, allowing the garment to slide down her arms and puddle on the floor. With a quirk of her brow, she walked from the room, knowing he'd follow.

She wanted him in her bed. She wanted to pull him just a bit deeper into her personal space. Little by little, she wanted him to realize that she meant business. Seduction came in all forms and Mia planned on using them all to get her man.

The couch rustled and she didn't have to turn to know he was only steps behind. She padded down the hall into her master bedroom. The evening sun glistened in her high windows, casting a pale glow onto her bed.

By the time she'd removed her mound of silk throw pillows and turned, Bronson stood in the doorway, gloriously naked. Mia extended her hand, inviting him to join her.

He closed the space between them, taking her hand in his. And as they came together, Mia knew in her heart this is where she was meant to be, where they were meant to be.

Bronson kissed her with so much passion, so much hunger, Mia nearly wept with anticipation. There was no way this man could be so giving and caring and only have physical feelings for her. She refused to believe it.

Grasping his broad shoulders, Mia eased down onto the bed, pulling him with her. She sank into the duvet, reveling in the delight of his weight on top of her.

He pulled up as if to move. "The baby?"

"Is fine," she assured him. "You're not hurting either one of us. I like you here."

Gently, he eased back down, trailing kisses over her face, her neck, her collarbone. Mia slid her hands up and down his muscular back as she lifted her knees.

In one smooth, toe-curling move they were one. Mia held tight to this man she was coming to care about more and more. She knew it wasn't a stretch to say she was falling in love with him.

Perhaps that was just the baby situation talking, but she didn't think so. He was caring, though cautious. He was loyal to everyone in his life and expected the same in return.

She'd tried to steel herself from falling for Bronson. Good Lord, considering his past, she didn't blame him for having trust issues. But that vulnerability beneath his alpha exterior had her melting, and she could see, could feel, that he was coming around. If he truly didn't believe her, he wouldn't be with her so much. And if she didn't think he had feelings for her—beyond sexual feelings—she wouldn't let him sleep with her.

Mia would prove, beyond a shadow of a doubt, that she wasn't lying about her feelings for him or about the baby.

But as pleasure consumed her, a niggling thought invaded her mind. She was lying, and that lie did involve Anthony.

Bronson took Mia's hand as he led her into the doctor's office for the ultrasound. The test was delayed for a week because the ultrasound tech had been ill, which irked Bronson, but here they were and Mia was fifteen weeks pregnant. He'd seen the little stars on her calendar hanging by the fridge. Every Thursday had a star with a number. He knew Mia was excited about the baby. And he hated to be pessimistic, but he had to rein in his own excitement until he knew for sure where he stood.

A part of him screamed that she was not lying, would never lie to him. But another part kept butting in and reminding him of the last woman who claimed to be carrying his child. Why couldn't he separate the two in his mind?

They took a seat in the private waiting room until it was their turn, which wasn't very long. As they went into the ultrasound room, Bronson helped Mia step up onto the table.

"Good afternoon," the tech said, coming in right behind them. "Feeling okay, Mia?"

Mia nodded. "Morning sickness has been gone for about a month, and I've never felt better."

The tech smiled as she laid Mia back and pulled her shirt up to her bra. "You're into your second trimester. Most women have a huge burst of energy during this time. No cramping or anything?"

"Not anymore."

Bronson stood beside the table, and when the tech put the scope on Mia's stomach and pointed to the screen, his heart literally constricted. He grabbed Mia's hand as he looked at the small, beating heart.

"I'll take some measurements to be sure of the due date, but it looks like your baby has a nice, strong heartbeat."

Bronson looked down to Mia, who was staring at the screen with watery eyes. "That's so amazing," she whispered.

The tech tapped a few buttons, moved the scope and tapped some more. "You're exactly fifteen weeks and one day. Looks like your due date is Valentine's Day."

Good Lord, that seemed so far away. This was just the start of September.

"A Valentine's baby?" Mia asked. "How appropriate, since I love her so much already."

The tech laughed. "We can schedule your next appointment for one month out and at that time we'll see if we can determine the sex of the baby. Assuming you want to know."

Mia looked to Bronson. "I'd like to. Would you?"

The sex? That would make this child all the more real to him, but as he glanced up at that little beating heart, he knew he was already sucked in. This baby was real and, he hoped, his.

"I'd like that," he said.

Mia's smile spread across her face. Between seeing this child and spending so much time with Mia lately, he was starting to fall into a role he wasn't sure he was ready for. And he was beginning to see Mia as the honest woman his mother had always claimed she was.

The tech wiped off the gel she'd put on Mia's slightly

rounded belly. "The receptionist will make that appointment on your way out."

Once they made the appointment and left, Bronson settled Mia in the car.

"Would you like to go out for a late lunch?" he asked.

"I'd love to, but I've got so much I need to do. Can you just drop me off at the main house?" she asked.

Disappointment speared through him, not something he expected. "Sure."

Mia stared down at the glossy black-and-white pictures the tech had given them. "I don't know that I'll get much done today. I may just have to look at our baby."

Our baby. He was getting used to those words.

"If you show those to my mother, I guarantee nobody will be working."

"I wasn't sure you'd want me to show them."

Bronson spared her a glance, hating how he always saw uncertainty in her eyes. "She knows we went."

He didn't want to admit that his mother had no doubts about this child's paternity. How could the woman be so sure? Granted Mia never gave him reason to doubt her. But in his mind the black mark against her was her relationship—whatever it may be—with Anthony Price.

"It's okay, Bronson. I don't mind keeping these to myself. I understand that you don't want her to get attached yet."

Mia's words sent an ache through him. He knew she wanted to share her excitement. After all, she really had no one else in her life.

And that right there was all the more reason for her to try to trap him into a family.

Dammit, he wished he weren't so cynical, but he had to be careful. He hated the thought of more scandal coming to his family.

Eleven

Déjà vu?

Bronson slammed the paper down onto the dark wood tabletop. He'd come to Saturday brunch at his mother's and had been greeted with today's "news"—a picture of him and Mia coming out the back door of the doctor's office. As if the image of Mia, a hand protectively on her belly, with him at her side weren't telling enough, the damning article went on to talk about "Dane's second chance at a family" and Mia "bed hopping from one Hollywood hot-shot to another."

This was the only drawback to his career. He couldn't even have a private life. Of course, after Mia's rumored affair with Anthony, she was great fodder for the media, as well.

"I'm sorry, Bronson."

Bronson turned from his cushioned chair to see Victoria standing next to him. As always, she appeared the picture of chic with her wraparound, sleeveless navy dress, gold jewelry and perfectly coiffed blond hair held back by her sunglasses.

Her eyes darted back down to the paper. "I just saw that earlier and tried to reach you, but my call went to your voice mail."

"Don't be sorry, Tori." Bronson came to his feet, placing a peck on his sister's cheek. "It's not your fault the media sniffed out this story. It was bound to happen. I just hope they leave Mia alone."

Victoria took a seat next to him and smiled. "I knew you cared for her."

"Yes," he said cautiously, because Victoria always had love on the brain. "I care. We're not planning a wedding or even playing house together. But I do care."

A little more than he was comfortable with.

Victoria waved a hand in the air. "I know you like to keep your feelings to yourself, so I won't say I told you so when you propose."

"Propose?"

Bronson groaned as he turned to see his mother only a few feet away. "No. There's no engagement. Tori's just fantasizing. Again."

Olivia kissed both her children on the cheek before taking a seat at the patio table under the bright California sun, shielded by a vibrant orange umbrella.

"Well, I for one would be all for bringing Mia into the family," Olivia declared. "She's a wonderful woman."

This was not what he was in the mood for today. He'd already lost sleep the past several nights over conflicting feelings for Mia. He needed to work this out on his own without his mother or sister influencing him. For pity's sake, he was a grown man who produced multimillion-dollar blockbusters. Surely he could decide how to handle a petite, Italian beauty who had his stomach in knots.

"I've drawn up a budget for the film," he told his mother, stopping midthought when the waitstaff approached because only three people knew about this project and they were all sitting at this table.

"Not a subtle change of subject, but a necessary topic." Olivia smiled up at the waitstaff as the two ladies brought out carts complete with soufflés, fresh fruit, breads and juice. Once they were out of earshot, she spoke again. "Have you chosen a director?"

"I've got two in mind." He took his napkin and placed it in his lap. "I'd like to discuss that with you."

"Allow me to throw my choice in." Olivia leveled her gaze at Bronson. "Anthony Price."

Victoria's audible intake of breath could barely be heard over the ringing in his ears. He set his cup of juice on the table, wishing for something a little stronger in his glass if this was the way his day was going to go. First the newspaper and now this preposterous request from his mother? She couldn't be serious.

"Hear me out," Olivia said, sitting straight up in her seat. "I have something important to tell you both, something that no one knows, and I'd prefer it stay that way."

Every nerve ending in his body prickled as he glanced at Victoria, who seemed to be just as nervous about this impending declaration as he was.

"I've had some tests that have come back unsatisfactory, according to my doctor." She looked from Victoria to Bronson. "I don't expect this to be anything more than a nuisance, but I am having further testing to rule everything out."

"What tests? What symptoms are you having?" Victoria asked.

"You've gotten a second opinion, right?" Bronson asked at the same time.

That genuine smile that had won her Oscars and worked its way into the hearts of millions spread across her face. But Bronson didn't care about the audiences who'd come to love her. This was his mother, and if her health was in jeopardy, he wanted her healed. Now.

"This is why I didn't want you two to know," she told them. "I don't want you to worry, and I don't want you to look at me the way you are now. I assure you, I feel fine, and I'm convinced this next round of tests will prove the others wrong.

"I've been having some slight chest pain, and I just attribute it to stress. My stress test came back a bit off, and the doctor wants to go in a take a look."

"When?" he asked.

"Monday."

Bronson tried to grasp that his mother wasn't invincible, as he'd thought. He'd been so self-absorbed lately, he'd ignored his mother and sister, trying to get his own life under control. Fear squeezed his chest as he stared at the woman who'd been his rock and source of strength for so long.

Which is why he had a hard time trying to comprehend what this had to do with Anthony Price.

"I'll clear my schedule," Victoria told her. "But what does Anthony have to do with any of this?"

Something flickered in Olivia's eyes, something he couldn't identify, which both worried and irritated him. She was hiding something.

"This medical nuisance has had me thinking." She looked Bronson dead in the eye. "You're the best producer in the business. No question. You cannot deny that Anthony is the best director. I want the best for the film we've written loosely based on my life, and I want you and Anthony to bury this animosity long enough to make this the best film ever."

Fury burned through him. "Why are you so insistent? There's more to this than your medical scare."

Olivia reached for the butter and began to layer a very minimal amount onto her freshly baked banana bread. "This will be my last film, Bronson, and this is what I want."

"Mother," Victoria piped in. "You're not retiring. Don't even suggest this is the last film you'll do."

"Darling, as much as I love to be in front of the camera, it's time for me to call it quits. I want to go out on top, and what better way than with my own story?"

Bronson stared down at the newspaper with the headline that continued to mock him.

He'd certainly had better days.

"You know why I hate Anthony. Asking him to work on this film is unacceptable." Bronson came to his feet. "We'll discuss directors after your appointment Monday, once we see what the doctors say. Until then, this topic is closed." He turned to Victoria. "See you later, Tori."

Walking away, Bronson didn't know where to go from here. He needed to calm down from his mother's request, he needed to grasp that his mother may have a heart problem and there wasn't a damn thing he could do about it.

But first things first. He needed to go see Mia and talk to her about that damning picture on the front page of the newspaper.

Mia couldn't believe the headline. She hadn't heard from Bronson, but she knew he'd be up having brunch with his mother and sister. She'd so hoped this pregnancy wouldn't get out until they were ready. The last thing she wanted was to cause more heartache for Bronson or to have the progress she'd made in getting him to open up encounter a setback.

She had a feeling he'd be dropping by after his brunch with his family. What she didn't have a clue about was the mood he'd be in when he arrived.

Rubbing the swell of her baby bump, Mia tried to relax by the pool. She'd donned her black string bikini, not caring that her waistline was expanding more quickly than she'd expected. Her cell sent out a shrill ring, jarring her from her thoughts. Why hadn't she left that thing inside?

Her fingers felt along the chaise until she found the phone tucked by her thigh. "Hello?"

"Tell me this isn't true."

Mia sat up, sliding her sunglasses onto the top of her head as Anthony's low voice interrupted her thoughts. "You saw the paper."

"You're not carrying Bronson's baby, Mia. Tell me you're not."

"I can't do that."

"You two have gotten close," Anthony said. "Obviously closer than I thought you would. You didn't…"

Mia came to her feet. "I didn't tell him, Anthony. I told you I wouldn't."

His frustrated sigh resounded through the phone. "How did you get entangled with him at all? I warned you, Mia. You knew what a ladies' man he was."

She tried to block that from her mind, especially since she was falling in love with that "ladies' man."

"I can't stop my feelings, Anthony. You of all people know that."

He let out a bitter laugh. "I'm not talking about my rocky marriage. I'm worried that you're getting in over your head here."

Touched, Mia turned toward the beckoning, clear water

of her pool. "I assure you, I've got everything under control."

"So when are you due?"

"Valentine's Day."

"Really? That seems so far away."

Mia glanced at her belly. "I have a feeling it'll be here before we know it."

"You sound happy."

She couldn't help the smile as she clutched her cell. "I really am. I'm not sure where we're going, but I'm happy and for now that's enough."

"Just don't sell yourself short."

Mia pulled her sunglasses back down to block the bright rays. "When will you talk to Olivia?"

The pause of silence didn't surprise her. She knew this was more than likely all he thought about. Well, that and how to keep his marriage intact.

"Anthony?" she urged. "You have to talk to her. I know this is your place to tell her, but I've gotten in deeper with this family. It's way beyond employer/employee, and it's putting a strain on me that I can't afford."

"I'd already decided to call her. Charlotte will be gone next week with some friends at our Tahoe home, so I'm going to call Olivia and set up a time to chat."

"You tell me when and I'll make sure her schedule is clear that day," Mia assured him. "I know it will be hard, but I really think it's for the best."

"I know it is. I just don't know what to say."

Mia sighed, not envying his position—or Olivia's, for that matter. "I'm sure once you tell her you know, she'll do all the talking."

Anthony talked for another few minutes while Mia listened. She knew he had no one else to talk to about this because he hadn't even told his wife. He'd claimed he didn't want to add any more of a strain on Charlotte and their marriage. She was already so sick of all the Hollywood hype. How would she react when he told her he was the biological son of Hollywood's Grand Dane?

Once she hung up with Anthony, she felt a bit more confident now that he'd assured her he was going to confront Olivia. She prayed the outcome wouldn't cause an explosion. She prayed even harder that Bronson would try to see a new side to Anthony and not hate her for keeping the secret.

Mia set her sunglasses and cell on the chaise and dove into the refreshing water. She loved relaxing by the pool and didn't feel the least bit guilty for spending her day doing absolutely nothing. A girl deserved a little "me time" every now and then. And with all she had on her plate right now, she most certainly deserved it.

The cool water calmed her as she swam a few laps. The doctor had told her she should continue any forms of exercise she normally did and not worry about too many activities.

"Too bad I don't have my trunks."

Mia jerked to a stop in the pool, sending the water rippling around her. "Bronson. I thought you were at brunch."

The tension practically radiated off his stiff shoulders, the muscle ticking in his jaw and the clenched fists in the pockets of his designer jeans.

"I was," he told her. "But this looks like much more fun."

Okay, so he didn't want to discuss what was wrong. She could take the hint, but that didn't mean she'd let it go for good or that his lack of openness didn't hurt her feelings. She longed for the day when he could talk to her without feeling as if she was going to double-cross him.

"You don't need a suit to get into my pool," she told him,

reaching behind her neck to undo the strings. "I'm game if you are, Mr. Dane."

A wicked smile spread across his lips. "I never was one to give in to peer pressure."

She flung her top, hitting him square in the chest with a sloppy, wet smack. "But you will now."

"I always said I'm willing to try anything."

And within seconds he joined her in the pool wearing only a tan and a smile.

Bronson drove home, top down on his sporty Mercedes, and reflected on the bits and pieces he'd overheard of Mia's conversation with Anthony. Obviously, this was Anthony's first inkling about the pregnancy.

A sharp pain had stuck in his chest when he'd come upon Mia's patio and overheard her telling Anthony something about keeping her word and clearing a schedule— Bronson assumed that meant his mother's schedule.

Did this have something to do with the film he and his mother were working on? Surely Mia and Anthony didn't know about that.

So what else would Mia need to clear Olivia's schedule for? And what the hell did Anthony have to discuss with his mother? Had she already told him about the film?

Something was going on, and Bronson had a sickening feeling that whatever it was, he wasn't going to like it.

Now more than ever, he intended to keep Mia close. Every part of him wanted to believe her. In fact, he had started to, but how could he be so certain after overhearing that conversation?

He had to get her away from here. They needed some one-on-one time where he could tap into those honest feelings of hers and see just where they stood on the loyalty platform. He wanted to build from there, but he could go no further until he knew why she was having private conversations with his enemy.

But first he'd have to lay himself on the line and hope he didn't get burned again.

Twelve

Monday morning Mia knew something was up. Olivia, Bronson and Victoria all said they'd be unreachable for the next few hours. Well, Bronson told Mia she could call in an emergency, but other than that, the three were out of commission for the day.

What was going on? Had Anthony decided to talk to Olivia early and now they were all in a family meeting?

Mia didn't know, and honestly, she didn't want to know. She just wanted to do her work and try to remain stress-free so she could have the healthiest, happiest baby ever.

And just like every other time she thought of the baby, she began to daydream. As always she chose the best features of Bronson and her. Not just physical, but character traits, too.

She hoped the baby had her Italian skin tone and dark hair with Bronson's blue eyes. She hoped their child had strength and determination from both of them. The classy, regal style of Olivia and the romantic and creative side of Victoria.

Mia's desk phone rang, and she pulled herself from the fantasy and remembered she was at work. Alone, but still at work.

"Hello."

"How fast can you pack?"

Mia smiled at Bronson's low, sexy tone. "Pack for what?"

"A trip. Five days and the destination is a secret. I have clothes at your service. All you need is essentials."

Was he for real? Who did this ever happen to?

"Well, I'm working today and for the next several days. And I thought you were not available to take calls right now."

Bronson laughed. "Our plans finished sooner and better than we'd hoped. I'll fill you in on the plane. I've already gotten you a hall pass from your demanding employer, so when can you leave?"

If he was that anxious to get her somewhere, hopefully alone, then she could be ready five minutes ago.

"I'll be ready in thirty minutes," she told him.

"I'll send my driver and meet you at the airport."

And with that he hung up.

Mia stared at the handset for a second before she burst out laughing. Sometimes that man just amazed her. A surprise trip complete with wardrobe? Did he even know what size her swelling body wore?

If her waistline continued to grow the way it was, she'd be going to Omar the tent maker to get her fall and winter wardrobe.

Mia saved the spreadsheet she was working on and shut off her computer. She couldn't get to her cottage fast enough to pack.

By the time she'd pulled her suitcase out and thrown in necessities—and sexy lingerie was the first necessity—she still had ten minutes to spare. She double-checked everything, including her passport, just in case, as the driver pulled up and took her bags.

Giddiness swept through her on the ride to the airport. Were they going on a cruise? Maybe a trip to Aruba? Oh, she hated waiting. Did the man not know how rude dangling the proverbial carrot was? Patience had never been her strong suit.

Okay, so that was a trait she didn't want to pass down to the baby.

At nearly five months along, Mia couldn't wait for the next few weeks to fly by so she could find out the sex of the baby. Back to that waiting game again.

The driver pulled into the private section of the airport and there was Bronson standing next to his jet, talking with a man she assumed was the pilot. A thrill of anticipation shot through her. Spending time alone with Bronson anywhere on earth would be fine with her, but the thought that he'd gone to the trouble to keep a surprise really threw her for a loop. Did she dare hope he was falling for her and not just feeling obligated to spend time with her for the baby's sake?

Bronson opened her door as the driver got her bags and passed them on to the pilot.

"Glad you're quick," he told her, kissing her cheek. "You ready?"

She smiled. "For you to tell me where we're going, yes."

"Oh, you'll find out soon enough. I just hope you're as excited as I think you'll be."

"I'm getting five days off to spend with you and not work? I'm already excited."

Bronson led her up the stairs of the private jet, and she settled into her plush leather seat. "How long is the flight?"

"Long enough for us to eat, sleep and have a stop to refuel before we arrive to our destination. I already called your doctor to clear your travels." He smiled as he looked down at her. "I thought this would be a good time for us to discuss baby names."

Mia froze, fastening her seat belt. "Baby names?"

"Yeah." He took the seat across from her and leaned forward, taking her hands in his. "The baby has to have a name. And I have to admit this is something I've been thinking about a lot lately."

Was he serious? Was he really ready to have their first parentlike discussion? Could he actually want this family to work?

Great, now she was going to tear up all because he was whisking her away and wanted to talk baby names.

"I didn't think you'd want to be that involved until you knew…"

"My involvement is inevitable." He kissed her hand. "And I want to do this. This baby will be an important part of the Dane legacy."

Did that mean he believed her now? Did she dare hope he'd quit lumping her together with his ex-fiancée, who'd betrayed him? Could they be more?

"Mr. Dane. We are ready for takeoff," the pilot said over the loudspeaker. "If you both would take your seats and buckle up, we'll be in the air in minutes. Beautiful, clear day. Should have a smooth flight."

Bronson fastened his seat belt and sat back. "So what do you think of the name Herbert?"

Mia's gaze darted to his, only to find him laughing. A humorous side? Who knew? This was going to be an interesting flight.

* * *

Bronson watched Mia's eyes light up at his joke. He only hoped he hadn't offended her and she didn't have some long-lost friend with that name.

"I know you've thought of names," he told her as the plane began to taxi down the runway. "I'll bet you've even scribbled some down to see what they look like."

"Maybe just a few." Mia laughed. "This is a big deal. We'll live with this name for the rest of our lives—and so will the baby. I want something classy and timeless, but not far out there."

Every day that passed, he was coming to think of this baby as his own. He couldn't pinpoint when he'd let the unknown override his feelings for this baby. Somehow Mia had not only pulled him into her web, but into this innocent baby's, as well.

And his mother and Victoria always questioned him about the child—that didn't help. Those two were so willing to look past everything and believe the best of Mia.

Couldn't they see how this would crush them if Mia was lying? Oh, he'd love to believe Mia, love to know he had a second chance at being a father. Love to know that this woman he was coming to care more and more about was not deceitful.

Truth was, he was ready to jump from the pessimistic ship he'd been sailing and get onboard with his family. But he also had to remain realistic to keep his heart from taking another beating.

"I have this feeling the baby is a girl," she went on. "So I've been thinking more girl names."

Bronson smiled. He could easily see Mia holding an infant in her likeness with dark hair, flawless Italian skin and those midnight eyes that looked straight through to your heart. His own heart constricted at the thought.

"Such as?" he asked as the plane lurched into the air.

She crossed her legs, smoothing her skirt down over her thighs. "Well, what do you think of Katharine or Audrey?"

"Classic movie stars, loved by millions."

Mia's silky laugh floated through the plane. "Get your mind off films for a minute. We're talking baby names. I want a name that will carry her from childhood to adulthood. Something strong, yet feminine."

"You're that sure it's a girl?"

She bit at her bottom lip, the lip he was dying to kiss. "I'm not sure, but maybe I'm just hoping."

Honestly, he didn't care, so long as the baby was his. Damn, he was going to be heartbroken if...

"Hey, you didn't tell me what was going on with your mom and sister this morning." Mia's brows drew together in worry as she leaned forward in her seat. "Everything okay?"

Bronson sighed, not wanting to think about the fact that after she came out of her same-day surgery with glowing reviews from the doctors, his mother had again asked him to consider Anthony as the director.

"My mother had a heart cath this morning."

Mia jerked up in her seat. "Oh, Bronson. I had no idea. She's never said a word to me that she was having cardiac issues. Is she okay?"

Bronson knew Mia's love for his mother was genuine and that only added to his confidence that she was trustworthy. And he was starting to care more for her than he ever intended.

"Her stress test showed something was off, so this was just a precaution. I assure you, she's fine and the doctor said she looks perfect."

Mia's visible sag of relief warmed him all over. She loved his family without question. But how would his heart take it if she was lying? He was getting in deeper every day and couldn't emotionally afford to lose her.

No, no. He didn't want love or any such emotion to be involved. No way was he ready for anything like that.

"Tell me where we're going," she begged. "Just a hint."

He'd gotten her this far, might as well give in. He'd always been a sucker for a woman begging.

"Tuscany."

Mia's eyes widened a split second before they misted. "Where my…"

He leaned across, taking her hands in his. "I know that's where your family was from. I thought you might want to see your birthplace before you begin your own journey as a parent."

"Bronson," Mia whispered as one lone tear trickled down her cheek. "I've never felt so appreciative or grateful. I don't know what to say."

Moved by her honest emotion, he unbuckled his seat belt, shifting to sit next to her and buckling in there. "You don't have to say anything. I've wanted to do this for you, but when Mom dropped this bombshell of her procedure the other day, I had to wait to see if we could still go. I wasn't sure what was going to happen with her."

Mia's delicate hand cupped his cheek. "You're the kindest man I've ever known. Our baby is going to have the best father."

Bronson swallowed the lump in his throat, grabbed Mia's hand and kissed it. "I have other surprises while we're there, but I refuse to tell you. Those you will have to wait for."

Mia sniffed, laid her cheek against their joined hands and smiled. "You've given me more than I'd ever hoped for."

He knew she wasn't just talking about the trip, but the

baby. A baby he could hardly deny any longer was his. He'd been sliding down a slippery rope since he found out Mia was expecting and he was hanging on by a strand.

He needed to know more about her on a personal level. Needed to try to develop the trust he so desperately wanted to have.

Mia's first impression of Tuscany was everything she'd dreamed. Rolling green hills, beautiful villas on hillsides and a sense of calm and serenity. Sunshine kissing the tops of trees, roads wet after a brief shower. And the beauty made that nineteen-hour plane ride worth every minute.

"How far is our villa?" she asked once they were settled into the car Bronson had rented.

"No villa."

"Are we camping in a tent?" She laughed.

Bronson smiled as he wound through the narrow streets. "I've rented a castle."

"A *castle?*" Mia tried to grasp the implications of that. "You're kidding."

"Not at all."

Mia watched the old city fly by. "But this was such short notice. How did you manage a room in a castle?"

He threw her a look as if to say, "Look who you're dealing with."

"We didn't get a room," he told her, turning back to the road. "The entire castle is ours until Friday."

Mia eased deeper into her seat. This man was nothing short of amazing. He'd gone through some trouble to whisk her away to the town in which her parents had met, fallen in love and started their young family. He'd rented an entire castle all to be alone with her. She didn't believe he went through all this just to sleep with her again.

He cared for her—that much was obvious. But did he

love her? Mia didn't know and had a feeling he was unsure himself. She had to be patient and let him figure out on his own where he wanted this to go.

When he pulled into the drive that wound up the hill, Mia gasped. "This is beautiful, Bronson."

"We used some of the grounds in a film I produced about five years ago. I've always wanted to stay here but never found a reason to."

Until now.

The words hung in the air just as if they'd left his lips. A wave of giddiness swept through her. Yes, he was falling in love with her. The emotions may be slow in coming, but they had started taking root in his heart. Of that she was sure.

"Every castle has a name," he informed her as he parked the car. "Welcome to Castello Leopoldo."

Mia didn't wait for him to come around and open her door, she hopped out and took in the Old World beauty. Light brick and stone with vines wound up and over the entryway. She could almost sense the magic from this place and couldn't wait to see what awaited them inside.

Bronson came up beside her. "There are eleven baths and ten bedrooms."

Mia glanced at him. "Are all those rooms on the agenda?"

With a quick kiss on her lips, Bronson murmured, "Count on it."

Thirteen

Mia stretched, smiling at the memory of how Bronson had already started making good on that multiroom promise.

Silk sheets swished softly as she shifted her bare legs. Bright rays slashed through the opening in the drapes and slanted sunlight across the bed.

Mia rolled on her side, tucking her arm beneath her head as she stared at a peaceful, sleeping Bronson. Dark lashes feathered his skin, a wisp of black hair fell over his forehead and those talented—mercy, were they talented—lips parted ever so slightly.

Swallowing a lump of fear, reality set in. She knew Anthony would be talking to Olivia this week. By the time she and Bronson returned from their romantic getaway, decades worth of secrets would be exposed and one by one the details would trickle out, giving the media the story of the century.

And leaving Bronson...what? Brokenhearted? Bitter? Destroyed?

As she studied his face, his bare shoulders and chiseled chest, she knew without a doubt she'd fallen in love with him and would do anything in her power to make sure he knew she was here for him.

But would he see her as a liar? Would he feel betrayed that she'd known the secret and hadn't told him?

How had she come to be wedged so tightly in the middle of this mess?

A flutter in her stomach made her gasp. Her hand flew over her abdomen as the light movement tickled her from the inside.

She jerked up in bed, laughing as she experienced her baby's first movement.

"What? What's wrong?"

Mia turned to Bronson, who'd sat up beside her. "Nothing. Everything is perfect. I just felt the baby move."

His eyes widened and darted to her stomach. "Are you serious?"

Mia nodded. "I'd read where the first signs of life are just a little flutter, and I felt it twice since I woke up. This is so amazing. I've never experienced anything like it."

Bronson's gaze came back up to hers. "Thank you."

Everything in her stilled. "For what?"

"For being you," he told her, moving in to wrap an arm around her and guide her back down. "For loving this baby so much the light shines in your eyes. For being genuine and honest."

Closing her eyes at the irony of his words, Mia forced herself to keep quiet about the secret. It wasn't her place to tell. Anthony and Olivia needed to work it out first.

"I do love this baby," she told him, looking back up into his blue eyes. "And I love you."

Bronson didn't stiffen as she thought he would at her declaration. Instead a flash of pain shot through his eyes a second before he closed them, as if to keep the hurt away.

Mia cupped his cheek, softly kissing his lips. "I don't say that to cause you more confusion or pain. I say it because I want to be open about my feelings for you. I don't expect you to say anything. My love is a gift, free for you to take."

He reached up, holding on to her hand. "I care about you and this baby—more than I wanted to. But that's all I can give, Mia. All I have in me."

The war he waged within himself spoke volumes about his love for her. If he didn't love her, he wouldn't be so torn and apologetic, so caring and nurturing.

He gently kissed her lips, then eased back. "I have some very nice surprises for you today."

"I hope one involves clothes, since you told me not to pack any."

Desire filled those eyes as his gaze darted down to her bare chest. "Pity, but yes, clothes are involved."

Mia smacked his arm. "Tell me, you know I hate waiting."

"There's a suitcase for you in the first bedroom we were in last night. You'll find Victoria Dane original maternity clothes."

"What?" Mia nearly jumped out of bed, dragging the sheet with her. "Your sister made me maternity clothes? But she only does evening gowns and wedding gowns."

Bronson, in all his fabulous naked glory, stretched out on the bed with a smile. "I happen to know the designer personally, and she did it as a favor. There are only a few pieces because she didn't have time for much and because she will make more as the pregnancy goes along."

Mia laughed. "That was a very nice way around telling

me I'm going to be a whale, but I'm so overwhelmed with gratitude and surprise, I don't care."

"Do you want to go get the clothes or do you want to hear what else I have in store?"

Decisions, decisions. "I'm greedy. Tell me what else."

He rolled to his side, propping his head up on his hand. "I've arranged cooking lessons from Italy's top chef, Chef Ambrogio Ricci. He'll be here around noon."

His words sank in and Mia raced back to the bed, hopping up on her knees. "You're kidding! Oh, my God, Bronson. This is amazing. I can't believe you did all this for me."

One tanned finger trailed down her bare arm. "It's only nine. I think we have plenty of time for you to show your thanks before our guest arrives."

Mia moved the silky sheet aside. "I don't know," she said, shoving him down to straddle him. "I'm pretty thankful."

A wicked smile donned his face as she set out to show just how grateful she was.

All doubts about his love were cast aside. He may not be able to say the words, but his actions were telling.

And speaking of action…

Bronson put the finishing touches on one of the bedrooms they hadn't made use of…yet. He'd greeted Chef Ricci and introduced him to Mia, then he'd given the two of them some privacy in the gourmet kitchen.

While they'd been preparing something that had sent a tantalizing aroma through much of the first floor of the castle, Bronson set up an intimate table on the balcony of one of the bedrooms on the top floor.

The elation in Mia's eyes when he'd told her about the

cooking lessons had taken his breath away, much like the moment when she'd felt the baby move. Their baby.

Bronson laid an exotic purple lily he was lucky enough to find in one of the lush gardens across Mia's plate and swallowed the lump in his throat. He could do this. He wanted to do this. He wanted to be the father of her baby, he wanted to get to that place in his life where he was comfortable enough with her to express his feelings.

Of course, for that to happen, he had to address those feelings within himself. Love was too strong for him to admit right now, but he'd never felt this way about another woman. Never truly cared and put her needs first. But over the past twenty-four hours, he'd really come to see Mia for the honest, loyal woman he'd hoped she was.

Once Bronson set out one last surprise on the table, he went to see how the lessons were going.

He'd made several phone calls and actually got a little work done while Mia was learning how to make authentic red sauce, homemade noodles and tiramisu from the top chef.

The lesson should be drawing to a close, and Bronson was more than eager to have Mia all to himself again. He was ready to tell her that he believed her about the baby.

Bronson may not trust Anthony, but he did trust Mia, and he knew in his heart that Mia wouldn't have slept with a married man. Even though she still kept in contact with Anthony, Bronson's gut told him the two were merely friends. She truly was one of the most honest people he knew. Why hadn't he seen how genuine she was before? She wore that loving heart of hers on her sleeve.

He only hoped he didn't break it. His track record with love wasn't all that great. In fact, it sucked. And right now, this journey he and Mia were on scared him to death, but he'd never backed away from a challenge, or fear. Or love.

And if he was scared, he could only imagine how Mia felt. She literally had no one else. He had a family who loved him, and he knew he could turn to them at any time—something he'd always taken for granted until he saw a glimpse into Mia's life.

Just as Bronson reached the first floor, he saw Mia closing the front door, a huge smile spread across her beautiful face.

"I take it from your smile and the aroma that your lessons went well."

Mia turned to him, still beaming. "Oh, Bronson, that was one of the best experiences of my life." She closed the space between them and wrapped her arms around his neck. "I'll remember this forever. Thank you."

Bronson's cheek rested against her silky hair, and he couldn't help but smile, too. "You are more than welcome, but I did this for selfish reasons."

Pulling back, Mia quirked a brow. "Oh, really?"

"I wanted authentic Italian food and I didn't want to have to leave the castle to get it."

Mia playfully slapped at his chest and turned back toward the kitchen. And, as always, Bronson followed those swaying hips.

"Grab a plate and see if my lessons paid off," she told him, removing the lid from the pot of sauce.

"I have a better plan."

Bronson pulled out some bowls and poured sauce into one and the pasta into another. He grabbed the bread and laid everything on a serving tray. "Get your dessert and follow me."

"Where are we going?" she asked.

"Trust me."

Two words that had really come to mean so much in their relationship.

Relationship? He guessed that's exactly what they had, and he was becoming more and more comfortable with that notion. Actually, the idea had him smiling even more as he led the way to the third-floor bedroom where he'd set up the romantic table on the balcony.

"Bronson," Mia gasped as she stepped through the doorway. "This is beautiful."

He set the tray down on the dresser just inside the bedroom. "I thought you might like the view from up here. Besides, we haven't used this room, yet."

Mia set her tiramisu on the dinner table and moved into him. "I don't know what I did to deserve all this. Words cannot express just how thankful I am."

She slid an arm around his waist, leaned her head on his shoulder and looked out over the view of the rolling green hills and the breathtaking countryside.

"I'm all for your showing me your thanks if words aren't enough."

He slid his arms around her waist, encountering that slight belly bump he just couldn't quite get used to. Each time he saw it, touched it, a lump rose in his throat. He was falling in love with this child, with this woman. But what if something happened to one of them? He couldn't afford to go through that nightmare again.

"I have to tell you something," he whispered into her hair. "I know this baby is mine. I know it because I've come to know you. You're genuine, honest. I also believe that you and Anthony are friends—probably better friends than I'd like, but that's your business."

Mia looked up at him, her eyes swimming with unshed tears. "Bronson, you can't know what that means to me. I want us to have trust. I want to be able to give this baby stability."

"We will," he assured her.

He couldn't wait to show her the final surprise he had in store. More than once he'd almost let it slip, but he wanted to see the expression on her face when he revealed the gift he'd been working on.

Mia didn't want this moment to end. Wrapped in Bronson's arms, looking on to the Tuscan countryside, feeling the soft flutter of their baby in her belly, nothing else in life mattered right now. There were no problems, no secrets. Nothing to keep her from happiness.

But as he pulled away to assist her with her chair, reality set in. There *was* a problem and there *was* a secret. She wanted to tell Bronson, wanted to tell him while they were in this magical place where the outside world couldn't touch them. But she was bound by loyalty to another man to keep his secret, and no matter how deep the love she had developed for Bronson, she would never go back on her word.

Bronson moved the flower to the side of her plate before dishing out hefty helpings of pasta.

"You okay?" he asked.

She forced a smile. They were in this magical castle, and she refused to think about what would be waiting for them upon their return home.

"I'm fine," she assured him. "Just nervous about your trying my first authentic Italian meal."

As he came back with bread, Mia poured a glass of water from the pitcher he'd had on the table. "What's this?" She tapped on the stainless-steel bowl with lid.

"Open it," he told her, taking a seat across from her.

Mia lifted the lid, stared at the contents and laughed. "All green M&M's?"

He shrugged. "Just in case your homemade dessert didn't turn out, I knew you liked those."

Mia's heart swelled even more. There was no question

Bronson loved her. How many ways had he shown her? Did she need him to say the words? They would be nice to hear, but she knew he wasn't ready to say them, and his actions had seriously spoken louder than three simple words could.

But what she prayed for more than anything was that he trusted her. And that he would still trust her when he discovered the truth about Anthony. That he would come to her, let her comfort him and explain why she hadn't been able to tell him what she knew.

Because if she lost Bronson from her life, she truly doubted that she would ever find love like this again.

Fourteen

"Another surprise, Bronson?" Mia asked as she climbed into the sporty silver rental car.

After a night of passionate lovemaking and testing her scrumptious dessert in bed, Bronson woke her with orders to get dressed and be ready in an hour.

"Trust me," he told her as he started the engine. "You may love this surprise most."

"More than a castle getaway, the cooking lessons, my own bowl of green M&M's?"

He smiled, steering them down the narrow street. "More."

Now that had her even more intrigued. "Can you tell me what it is?"

Reaching over, he grabbed her hand and laughed. "You have really got to learn some patience, Mia."

"I will. Tomorrow. Now tell me where you're taking me."

The infuriating man merely laughed as he drove. They

traveled for nearly an hour before coming to a beautiful little town with bistros and specialty shops.

"What are we doing here?" she asked once he'd parked.

"Shopping."

Mia jerked around. "You like to shop?"

"Not really, but I love seeing you happy. We're looking for baby furniture."

Mia squealed. "Baby furniture?" She glanced out the window at the small, locally owned shops. "Do they have a furniture store here?"

"Even better. They have a store where you can custom-order your furniture and it's all made and shipped to you."

Was this a dream? And she'd thought in Cannes she'd outdone Cinderella. This was much, much bigger than anything she could've ever imagined.

"The owner has made some pieces for my mother and Victoria," Bronson told her as he unbuckled his seat belt. "I've never been to his store, but I've spoken with him on the phone a few times with this day in mind."

Unable to contain the excitement bubbling within her, Mia shoved open the car door. "Let's go."

Bronson came around, took her hand and led her to the store down the block. "I called Fabrizio yesterday and informed him we'd be in. He's fluent in English and is known worldwide for his baby furniture collection."

Anticipation spread through her as Mia entered the quaint store, a small bell chiming overhead. Sample pieces of intricate headboards made of solid oak sat along the wall. Tables of all shapes, sizes and various stains were all around them. Classy chairs and sofas upholstered in an array of fabrics anchored the room, drawing her eye to the middle-aged man coming toward them.

"Mr. Dane, welcome." The man closed the gap, shaking Bronson's hand. "And you're the lovely Mia. I'm so thrilled you chose to come here. It doesn't seem like that long ago I was building a crib for your parents."

Mia's breath caught as she risked a glance to Bronson, who merely smiled and nodded. He'd planned this. Love flooded her as she looked back to Fabrizio.

She slipped into Italian so easily. *"Avete conosciuto I miei genitori?"* You knew my parents?

The elderly man smiled. *"Ero un amico d'infanzia con il tuo padre."* I was childhood friends with your father.

Mia couldn't stop the tears from collecting. "I'm honored to meet you," she told him, switching back to English. "I'm even more honored you're going to make my baby's furniture."

"Oh, my pleasure. My Viviana and I had eight children of our own. There's nothing as special as welcoming a child into this world."

He motioned for them to follow as he made his way toward the back of the store. "Come into my office. I've pulled some books for you to look at. Some old designs, some new."

Mia followed the Italian man with a heavy accent and graying temples. Of course with eight kids, it was a wonder the man wasn't bald.

Mia rubbed the side of her belly as a little flutter tickled her. She couldn't wait to see her baby, to savor the treasure of motherhood and communicate with her child face-to-face.

They went into a small office where many binders and loose pictures were displayed across the desk. Mia took a seat in a cozy, curved, velvety chair and picked up one of the pictures.

"These are amazing," she murmured, truly taken aback by the beauty. "I've never seen anything like them."

"After Mr. Dane called me, I wanted to give you a variety." He leaned a hip on the edge of his desk. "If there's something you like in more than one picture, we can try to combine styles or colors. Whatever you like, I'll try to make it happen."

After several minutes of looking in silence, Mia choked up as she studied the perfectly round crib with a little pink canopy over the top. Easily she could see her baby snuggled in a deep slumber beneath the silky canopy.

As she looked through more pictures, Bronson remained standing, not saying a word. Did he want to distance himself from this? Was he just letting her choose because he still had doubts about whether this baby was his?

No. If he didn't believe he was the father, he wouldn't have done this for her and their baby. She had no doubt he was still frightened that something would happen to the child, but still, she wished he'd say something. Take some part in this decision.

Mia went back to the first picture that had captured her attention. The soft colors and delicate woodwork were appropriate for either gender.

"I want this one."

Fabrizio nodded with a smile. "Any changes you'd like made?" he asked.

"None. But I don't know if I'm having a boy or girl, so I'm unsure of the bedding."

"You can call me and let me know, or we can choose a unisex color for the bedding. There are so many nice materials for a universal crib."

Mia's mind worked overtime, thinking of the layout of her cottage, the way the windows let the morning sun in and how that would affect the color scheme.

"Could I see the materials and pick one for a boy and one for a girl and let you know?"

The man smiled. "Of course. It will take a few weeks for me to complete this design. But I'll try to have it ready in two weeks because you are a special client."

"We have an appointment in two weeks to learn the sex of the baby," Bronson told the man. "I'll give you a call."

"Fine." Fabrizio motioned for them to follow him out of the office and onto the showroom floor. "Now let's look at fabrics."

After choosing all the necessary materials and designs for either sex of the baby, Mia couldn't help but impose on Fabrizio another few moments to question him about her parents. This was the closest connection she'd had to them, other than the locket around her neck, and she wanted to hold tight to that thread of similarity.

Bronson stepped outside the office, giving them privacy, and Mia delighted in hearing childhood stories about her father, then about how he and her mother were so excited to be having a baby.

Mia choked up a few times, but Fabrizio was a gentleman and offered her a tissue as he continued reminiscing.

Before long, an hour had passed. Mia apologized and promised to keep in touch and send baby pictures once her little one was born.

Now more than ever Mia knew Bronson loved her. He'd purposely found this man who knew her father. He'd set up this meeting, this day, all so she could have that glimpse into her past as it collided with her future.

So many emotions whirled around inside her, and she just didn't know how to react. One thing was certain, though, she needed Bronson to still feel he could trust her once they returned home and he discovered the truth she'd been hiding from him. She hadn't come this far to lose him now.

JULES BENNETT   157

After lunch at a small bistro and some more shopping in the cute little specialty stores, Mia was thankful to be back at the castle and put her feet up.

"I had no idea a baby could zap so much energy from your body," she said, sinking into the leather sofa in the main living room. "This is all starting to seem so real. The baby, I mean."

Bronson laughed, settling in beside her. "You mean the morning sickness wasn't a sign of it being real?"

She shuddered at the thought. "Oh, yeah. That was real enough, but this trip, being here with you, feeling the baby move, picking out furniture. Everything just seems so... right."

As Bronson wrapped an arm around her, Mia settled in closer to his side. They only had one more day here, and Mia had so much she wanted to tell him. So much she needed him to see about her life so he would understand her actions when he discovered the truth.

She rubbed the scar on her hand, as if to draw courage from the fateful night that had changed her life, molding her into the person she was today.

"You know I'm not lying about this baby." Silence answered her, sending a stabbing pain through her chest. "I need to know you believe me, Bron."

"I do." His voice, thick with emotion, enveloped her. "I've been afraid to admit it for fear of losing another baby I loved, but I know."

Months' worth of worry, of fear, evaporated at his heartfelt declaration. He loved this child.

"I know this is probably hard for you, but I promise nothing is going to happen to this baby." Mia rested her hand on Bronson's denim-clad thigh. "I don't know how

to thank you for all you've done for me. Introducing me to
Fabrizio... I'll never be able to thank you enough."

"You don't have to thank me." He toyed with the ends of
her hair. "I care about you and this baby. I wanted you to
get a glimpse of your past. I have my family, and I'm glad
I got to show you a side of yours."

Mia glanced up at him. "You'll be a wonderful father.
You have such a loving family, and you're all so close. This
baby won't want for anything."

"My father passed away when I was ten," he told her.
"The media actually handled it better than my mother
thought they would by letting us have our privacy. I always
wanted to be like him. He was the man of the house, and it
didn't bother him at all that my mother was a Hollywood
icon. Some husbands would've been jealous, but he was so
proud of her."

Mia watched a play of emotions cross Bronson's face.
"I knew my career in the film industry would come before
anything, but once I had my footing, I wanted a wife, a
mother for my children, and I wanted to be my dad. De-
voted, loyal, loving."

Why couldn't he see he was all those things and more?

"I met Jennifer on a movie set and thought I'd found the
one," he went on, staring into the fireplace as if watching
the movie unfold before him. "Then she lost the baby. We
argued about everything. Looking back I know we weren't
compatible, but lust screws up the senses. She knew about
my feelings toward Anthony—hell, everyone in the industry knows we don't get along on set. She'd worked on a
film with him in the past and told me he was the father of
the child."

Mia's heart ached for him and for Anthony. This entire
fiasco between these two was, she feared, going to get a
whole lot worse before it got better.

"You know she was lying, right?" Mia asked. "I mean about Anthony. I can't say if she had an affair or not with someone else, but I know Anthony and I know how much he loves his wife. I've seen firsthand how hard he fights for their marriage."

Bronson snapped his gaze down to hers. "I never thought of her lying about the father, but when she threw that in my face—true or not—it shattered what little relationship we had left."

"I'm not her, Bronson." Mia lifted her hand, cupped his cheek and eased her body around just a bit more to face him. "I'm not lying to you. I assure you, Anthony and I are, and always have been, just friends. That's why I stopped working for him—because I saw the struggle he was going through with Charlotte, and I knew he loved her or he would've just walked away at the first sign of scandal."

Bronson's blue eyes, which never failed to impress her, studied her face. "I know you're not her. You're a fighter and stand up for what you believe. You're loyal and honest."

Tell him, the voice in her head practically screamed, but Mia couldn't do it. She couldn't betray the trust of a friend. She just had to believe that Bronson would understand her reasoning once the truth came out.

"I'm not sure what kind of mother I'll make," she told him, easing back down against his side. "I mean, I haven't had an example, and I've never really been around babies. One of my foster homes had a toddler, but I wasn't there long enough to get attached."

"You were bounced around a lot?"

Mia nodded. "Yeah. After my parents died, I was placed into four foster homes by the time I was ten. When I turned ten, I was placed in a home with other kids waiting to be adopted. I was there until I turned eighteen, and then I decided it was time to take control of my life and do something that pleased me. I had no one else to please or answer to."

"I'm amazed at the woman you've become, Mia, considering you were so young when your parents were killed."

Mia nodded, rubbing her scar. "Yeah. I was five."

He slid a finger alongside hers. "And that's where this came from?"

"I only had minor injuries, but my parents were killed. Sometimes life isn't fair," she murmured. "I may not be the best mother, but I will love this baby with every fiber of my being and always put her needs before my own."

Bronson moved in front of her, taking her hand in his. "I have no doubt you'll be a fantastic mother, Mia. I'm not worried about that one bit. You go into everything in life with excitement at full throttle and give 110 percent.

"That's one of the reasons I brought you on a getaway." He leaned forward, placing a soft kiss on her lips. "I want you to know that I believe you, that I trust you and that I want to see where this thing between us will lead. That's all I can offer, but I hope you'll be patient with me."

Love speared through her, nearly bursting to get out. She'd never, ever felt like this—so alive, so happy. She wrapped her arms around Bronson, choking back tears.

"Love is patient," she whispered in his ear. "I'm not going anywhere."

She eased back, noting the desire in his eyes, knowing hers matched his. Sealing the new milestone in their journey was logical, and Mia hoped every time they made love he could see, feel, just how much she did love him.

Bronson's strong hands slid up the skirt of the tunic-style dress Victoria had made for her. Warmth spread through her as he leaned in to capture her lips again, massaging her thighs.

Mia broke the kiss, coming to her feet. Gripping the

hem of the garment, she pulled it over her head and tossed it aside. Desire shot straight through her as Bronson's gaze slid up her body, pausing at her matching yellow bra-and-panty set.

"You always have the most amazing things on under your clothes," he told her, coming to his feet.

Mia slid his polo shirt off as he worked his jeans down and kicked them aside. He palmed her shoulders and tugged her toward him until she fell against his hard, solid chest. Mia looked up just as his lips came crashing down on to hers.

The swell of her belly brushed against him as their bodies molded together. Mia poured her emotions, her desires, her love into the kiss.

Bronson eased back, bent down and picked her up to carry her. "Where to?"

"Bronson, I'm getting too heavy for you to carry," she scolded. "Put me down."

"You've barely gained anything, and if I want to carry my family, I will."

Mia's eyes stung as she stared back at him. "Your family? In that case, take me anywhere you want."

Hope sprang to life within her. He thought of them as a family. Did he intend to make them a family in the legal way?

Oh, God. Her dreams of a family, a real unit, could come true and with a man she was totally in love with. She realized she'd never want a family with anyone but Bronson.

He carried her down the narrow, stone hallway out one of the back doors. "I want to make love to you outside, in the open, under the stars."

Mia knew there was no one around to see since the castle sat on a huge lot and they were the only residents.

He set her on her feet, wrapping his arms around her. "Look at me, Mia."

She lifted her face, knowing her love shone in her eyes.

"Know that I care for you, know that what is between us is real to me and that I'm giving all I can emotionally."

Mia smiled, holding his face between her hands. "I know, Bronson. I know more about you than you know about yourself. Make love to me."

With soft, tender touches, he kissed her as he rid her of her bra and panties. Once she stood wearing only a kiss of the moonlight, Bronson placed his hands on her belly. He leaned down, kissed her stomach and murmured, "I love you" to the baby.

Mia choked back tears, knowing he was taking a giant leap outside his comfort zone by declaring his feelings aloud. His vulnerability was now out in the open for her to see. Which told her right there that he trusted her—and possibly loved her, too.

Bronson came up to his full height, framed her face with his hands and kissed her, backing her up until her legs hit the outdoor sofa. He spun them around and took a seat, urging her down to straddle him.

Mia hovered with her face above his, looking into his eyes, needing him to know that her love was genuine. "I love you."

As they became one, Bronson's eyes closed. Mia leaned down to kiss him as he stroked his hands up and down her bare back. The crisp night air pricked her skin, sending even more sensations surging through her.

She tilted her hips, arching her back as she lifted her face to the night sky. Bronson's talented hands found her breasts and sent Mia over the edge. She cried out and let the climax spread through her.

In no time Bronson's body stiffened as he grabbed her

shoulders and pulled her back against him, capturing her mouth.

Mia held on to his shoulders as their tremors merged into one and knew that this was the man she was meant to spend her life with. There would be heartache, she had no doubt about that, but she intended to fight for him, for their family.

He loved her. Now she just had to pray that love was strong enough to get them through the next few days.

Fifteen

Once Bronson's jet landed back in L.A., Bronson dropped Mia off at her cottage because his mother had called his cell and told him to come to the house before going anywhere else. She assured him her health was fine, but they urgently needed to talk in private.

He hadn't told Mia about the message because he didn't want to alarm her. What else could be wrong? If her health was fine, what else could she have to discuss that was so important?

Even though his mother was a Hollywood icon, she'd never been one for personal drama. Twice in one week she'd needed to see him in private—that made him a bit nervous.

Bronson entered the main house, smiling at one of the staff as they passed each other on the wide, curved stairs. As he entered the grand study where his mother spent nearly all her time, he noticed two things right off the bat:

one, his mother had been crying and two, Anthony Price stood right next to her.

"What the hell is going on?" he demanded.

Olivia gestured toward the sofa where his sister sat. "Please, Bronson, sit with your sister. There's something you both need to know"

Remaining on his feet, Bronson eyed Anthony. "What's he doing in your house? Did you go around me and hire him for the project? We were supposed to discuss this when I returned."

Olivia's eyes, now misting back up, turned to Anthony. "No, this has nothing to do with the film."

A sickening pit bottomed out in his stomach. Nothing, absolutely nothing good was going to come from the next few minutes. Of that he was certain.

"Why are you upset?" he asked, fear of the unknown gripping at his chest.

"These are tears of joy," his mother assured him. "And a little of fear, I must say."

"Come sit, Bronson." Victoria shifted on the sofa and smiled. "I'm sure whatever Mom has to say is very important."

"If it's that important, maybe just family should be here."

Why was Anthony looking so…comfortable? What the hell did the man have to do with anything that his mother could have to say?

"Actually, that's precisely what I need to talk to you both about," Olivia said. "Family. Bronson, I want you to promise not to speak until I'm done talking."

He never, ever liked the sound of that, especially coming from his own mother. Who wanted to give up the right to interrupt when the conversation wasn't going in a satisfactory direction?

"Bronson?" she asked.

"Fine."

Olivia came to her feet, crossed the room to stand in front of the French doors that opened on to the patio. Silence settled into the room and Bronson knew his mother was having a hard time voicing her thoughts. Whatever she wanted to say obviously upset her.

And there was no script to follow in real life.

Olivia smiled. "I never thought this day would come. I dreamed of how I'd handle it, but I never thought it would be a reality."

Victoria reached over and grabbed Bronson's hand, and honestly he wanted that connection. Who knew what was going to come next from his mother's lips.

"I was at a pivotal point in my career nearly forty years ago," she went on. "I had one of the biggest roles of my life handed to me without an audition. The industry adored me. I had never been so alive, so happy. I was only twenty years old, and I was pregnant by a man I didn't love enough to marry."

Bronson drew his brows together, biting his tongue because that wasn't right. His mother was twenty-five when he was born, and he knew she'd loved his father.

"I panicked because I was not ready to be a mother. I was still working on my career and knew that if I had a baby, I wouldn't put his needs before mine. I admit I was selfish, but I also admit that an abortion was out of the question. I wanted this baby to have a good life, and I was wealthy enough that I could buy a private adoption and pay any lawyer and judge to keep this from leaking to the press.

"And I did."

Victoria squeezed Bronson's hand. Whether she was

scared or because she wanted him to keep his promise of silence, he didn't know.

"Anthony is the son I gave up for adoption."

"This is preposterous." Bronson came to his feet. "Price, what have you told my mother? Did you dig up this dirt on her about an adoptive child and now you're blackmailing her?"

Anthony shook his head. "What would I blackmail her for, Bronson? I have everything I want and I could buy anything else."

"Then what the hell *do* you want?"

Olivia stepped forward. "Bronson, calm down. I've known Anthony was my son from the moment I gave birth to him. I gave him up for adoption and kept track of him all this time. He's not lying, and quite honestly, I'm shocked he found out and came to me. I paid a lot of money to keep this hidden."

Anthony sighed. "It wasn't easy. I've had my attorneys and a detective looking for my birth parents for well over a year. I didn't think they'd uncover anything, but about nine months ago they did."

Nine months?

"You've known for all this time?" Bronson clenched his fists at his side. "Why wait this long to come forward?"

Bronson stared at the man he'd loathed for so many years. Now that he knew the truth, he noticed they had exactly the same eyes and facial structure…just like their mother.

Anthony ran a hand through his hair. "Honestly, my home life hasn't been the best, as I'm sure you've heard. I'm trying to work on my marriage, and I'm fumbling through assistants since mine came to work for Olivia."

Mia. Another time line perked Bronson up even more.

"Does Mia know about this?"

Anthony stared without saying a word, and dammit, Bronson knew.

How the hell could she keep something like this from him? Maybe this really was some scheme devised by Anthony and Mia.

The mother of his child.

One crisis at a time.

"So now what?" Bronson asked, turning to his mother. "I hope you don't expect me to accept him as my brother. I never liked him before, and I sure as hell don't like him now."

"Bronson," Victoria's soft, smooth voice cut through his anger. "Nobody is asking you to do anything. The truth is out there, now we just have to deal with it."

"The truth?" He laughed. "If Mother had been so worried about the truth, she would've told us years ago."

"And disrupt the only life Anthony had ever known?" Olivia interjected. "I made my choice to give him a better life, and I wasn't going to push my way back in. I couldn't afford to tell anyone."

"All these years Bronson and I feuded were hell on you, I'm sure," Anthony said to Olivia.

Olivia's eyes filled, and one tear slid down her aged cheek. "It was torture to see my children always at odds."

"This isn't happening," Bronson muttered to himself. "This cannot be happening."

"I assure you," Anthony said. "I'm no more thrilled that we're related than you are."

Bronson walked to his mother, angry at her for keeping something so…life-altering from him all these years, but at the same time heartbroken because he couldn't imagine giving up a child.

"Mom." He wrapped his arms around her. "I honestly don't know what to say here. I want to be angry with you, but I can see you're at war with yourself. I can't welcome him into the family. I just can't."

Olivia sniffed against his polo and nodded. "I know, son. My only wish is that you two will cease this feud and at least try to get along."

Bronson doubted that would happen, but he'd appease his mother. "I'll do my best."

He eyed Anthony over his mother's shoulder. The illegitimate brother stared back, a knowing look passing between them. Anthony wasn't any more eager to have Bronson for a brother, and that was perfectly fine.

Because this whole brother thing was a non-issue as far as he was concerned. What *was* a concern was Mia. The woman he'd made a baby with, trusted and started falling in love with.

She'd betrayed him even more than his mother—though he hated to call what his mother had done betrayal. She'd given up the child nearly forty years ago and had reasons for keeping it a secret.

Mia, though, had known from the second she'd stepped out wearing only a towel that he was Anthony's brother. And she'd never said a word. Never even hinted at the fact.

Bronson eased back, keeping an arm around his mother's shoulders. "What did you promise Mia for keeping silent about this?" he asked Anthony.

"Nothing. I asked her to keep this to herself until I had a chance to talk to Olivia."

Bronson laughed. "And she just agreed to it?"

The muscle in Anthony's jaw ticked, his dark eyes narrowed. "And here I thought you knew her. You know nothing about Mia if you have to ask that."

That's exactly what Bronson was beginning to see. Just how well *did* he know Mia?

He knew her body better than she did. He knew she lit

up like a child at green M&M's. Her culinary skills were amazing, and she kept the locket with a picture of her parents around her neck at all times so she could always have them with her.

That much he knew.

What he didn't know was how deep her love for Anthony ran—platonic or not. He didn't know if she truly had an agenda as far as he and his family were concerned and the pregnancy threw a wrench in her plans.

At this point he knew nothing except his life had just done a one-eighty and now his worst enemy was his brother and a woman he thought he knew was carrying his child.

"Leave Mia out of this," Olivia said. "If she knew, then I'm even more impressed with her for keeping this to herself."

"Impressed?" Bronson wasn't impressed at all right now. He was angry, hurt, betrayed. "After all she and I have been through, she should've told me."

"Loyalty is something Mia prides herself on," Anthony said. "And even though right at this moment you're angry with her, she'd be just as loyal to you if you asked her to keep something to herself."

Bronson turned toward Anthony. He was the dead last person Bronson wanted to have a conversation with regarding Mia.

"This changes nothing." Bronson narrowed his eyes. "You want to spend time with my mother and try to form some sort of bond, that's up to her. I'm not feeling very brotherly."

"Bronson." Victoria came to stand beside him, placing a delicate hand on his arm. "Don't say things right now that you don't mean. We've all sustained a shock. Let's just think this through, let it all settle and then we'll decide how to proceed."

He glanced down at his sister who had a loving heart for everyone. "Tori, my feelings won't change for him just because we share a mother. I've never trusted him, and I'm not going to be buddies with him. You and Mom are free to do what you want with this newfound relationship, but I want no part of it."

Unable to stay in the same room with the tension, the lies and the hurt, Bronson turned to leave.

"No," Anthony said. "I'll go."

Bronson looked over his shoulder. "What?"

His illegitimate brother crossed the room. "I'll go. You three have a lot to discuss and you don't need me here. I realize I'm not part of this family, and it's certainly not my intention to break anything up. I know this will take a lot of time to deal with."

Bronson was shocked at Anthony's gracious action, volunteering to leave. He wouldn't have thought the man would step aside at a time like this. Bronson was grateful... though he wouldn't admit it.

He nodded to Anthony, who then turned to Olivia. "I hope I can call or stop by again soon."

Olivia's face lit up as a smile spread across her face. "Anytime, my darling."

"Goodbye, Anthony," Victoria said with a tender smile.

Anthony spared Bronson one last look before leaving.

Bronson turned back to his mother. "You've always known?"

Olivia lifted her chin. "Yes, and I'm not ashamed of my actions because I'd do the same thing again to give my child the best start at life."

Anger, confusion and hurt spread through Bronson. He wished he had somewhere to place the blame, but he didn't want to castigate his mother. In his heart, he knew his mother had made the hardest decision of her life, and making her pay for it nearly forty years later wouldn't fix anything.

"Oh, Mother, I wish you'd said something." Victoria wrapped an arm around their mother's shoulders. "The pain you must've felt all these years with all the turmoil between Bron and Anthony. Why didn't you at least tell us? We never would've told a soul."

"Because if Anthony never came to me, I would've died with this secret." Olivia smiled at Victoria. "I do have him in my will, and I even had letters to each of you that you were supposed to receive if something happened to me. I gave specific instructions for you to read the letters well before the reading of my will so you wouldn't be as stunned."

"Letters, Mother?" Bronson asked, resting his hands on his hips. "I never took you to be afraid of anything, yet you couldn't tell us this?"

Those sparkling blue eyes that had dazzled the camera for decades turned to him. "To be honest, I didn't want either of you to be disappointed in me. I was human. I met a man I thought I loved, got pregnant and knew I was in no position to raise or care for a child properly. It wasn't until a couple years later I met your father, and I told him everything before we married. He tried to get me to reclaim Anthony then, but I couldn't do that. I'd given him up to a loving family, and I refused to tear them apart."

Bronson swallowed, unable to even fathom giving up a child. He'd lost one and thankfully had the chance to be a father again. But to willingly give the baby up so he could have a better life?

He wrapped his arms around two of the most important women in his life. "You're the bravest woman I know," he whispered to his mother. "I'm glad you don't have to carry this secret anymore. Just please don't expect me to change overnight."

Olivia clutched his shirt at his back and hugged him to her side. "I won't, son. But promise you'll try to make amends with Anthony. For me."

For his mother he'd try anything. But first he had another woman in his life to deal with.

Sixteen

Mia opened her door to a very tense, angry Bronson. The muscle ticking in his jaw, the thin lips and narrowed eyes were all directed at her.

Her heart stopped and she knew the secret was out. Now was possibly her one and only chance to salvage their relationship and prove that her love for him was never in question.

"You saw your mother?"

"Would you ever have told me, Mia?"

Mia's gaze darted down to her bare feet, then back up. "No."

"My mother said the same thing," he whispered. "Betrayal from all sides. This secret just gets better and better."

A flash of pain tore through Bronson's eyes before he pushed past her and entered her house. With a heavy heart and a sickening pit in her stomach, Mia shut the door and followed him.

"Your mother knew?" Mia asked, shocked.

He spared her a glance as he moved into her living area. "She's known the whole time."

Bronson stood looking out on to her patio, his back to her. "You want to tell me again that there was never anything between you and Anthony? Why your loyalty is stronger for your previous employer than the father of your baby?"

She would not fight. There was no reason to start arguing, Mia told herself. He was hurting and looking for a place to lay blame, and she was in the path of his destruction. She had to be strong to keep this relationship afloat on these rocky waters.

"I've never lied to you about my involvement with Anthony," she told him in a soft voice. "I love Anthony like a brother, and I saw him struggle with this secret. I happened to stumble across the information just about a week before I was set to leave and come work for your mother. I assure you, more than once I wished I'd never known the truth."

"But you did." He turned, hands on his hips. "You knew the truth that would change my life. You slept with me, made a child with me and professed your love for me all the while knowing this."

How could she deny anything?

"Yes."

He threw his arms in the air, his voice boomed through her house. "How can I trust what you say, Mia? How can I ever trust you to be open and honest with me? You of all people know how important family is."

Okay, that was low, but she refused to let him pull her into a fight, refused to throw away this family she'd already come to love.

"Bronson, family means everything to me, too." A soft

flutter slid through her stomach as her baby moved. "But this was not my secret to tell, and if Anthony had decided to never open up, then my spilling the secret would've ruined everything."

"Did you know he was going to talk to my mother?"

"Yes. He told me last week he'd be talking to her in the next few days."

Bronson's lids fluttered down, and a curse slipped through his lips. "So the whole time we were gone you knew what was happening back here?" he asked, directing those blue eyes at her.

Mia nodded. "I was so worried what we'd come home to, but I wanted that time with you, Bronson. I wanted that time with just us because I have fallen in love with you. Not because of the baby, but because of us."

Bronson laughed. "There is no us, Mia. *Us* implies a unit, and I'm not going to be part of a team where I can't trust my partner."

The burn in Mia's throat quickly spread to her eyes, but she wasn't giving up. She'd known going in this would be hard, but she had never been a quitter.

"If you look back, you'll see I did nothing to make you not trust me, Bronson. If you think that you can't see where this relationship would go, then fine. Walk out that door and don't look back. Don't give me a second thought. But I know you can't do that."

"Not when you're carrying my baby," he threw back.

Anger fueled Mia. "The baby may have brought us together, but this baby is not the reason I want to be with you or the reason I love you. And you cannot tell me you aren't in love with me, Bronson."

"I'm not."

"Now who's lying?" she whispered through tears. "You make love to me like I'm the most important thing in your life. You whisk me away to a castle for a week when I know you never take that much time off work. You surprise me with all of my favorite things and you take me shopping for custom-made, Italian furniture. Don't even deny those are signs of love."

That gaze bore into her, but Mia held her ground. Her future, their baby's future, was at stake.

"Leave if you want," she told him, praying he'd come to his senses. "But know that no one will ever love you as much as I do. No one will ever be as faithful and loyal to you as I will. And know that you are throwing away a family that would've made you a lifetime of memories."

The muscle in Bronson's jaw ticked as he stared her in the eyes. Tension-filled silence enveloped Mia, but she hadn't come so far in her own life by backing down from getting what she wanted.

"'Throwing away' implies I had something to begin with." Bronson stepped away from the windows and crossed the wood floor to stand before her. "Yes, we have a baby, but that's all. As far as I'm concerned, there's nothing else between us. There never was, and there never will be."

He brushed past her, careful to turn his shoulder so he didn't even come in contact with her. Mia stood stone-still as his shoes clicked on the tile in the foyer. She didn't even move when he opened the door and closed it.

It wasn't until the roar of his engine died that she sank back onto the couch. Tears slid down her cheeks, one chasing after the other. But Mia didn't feel defeated. She hadn't lost this fight yet, and she certainly didn't intend to.

Bronson just needed time to think. He needed time to adjust to all that had been thrown at him in one day. Mia couldn't expect him to deal with her when she had no doubt the relationship with his mother was probably now strained.

Mia's heart ached for Olivia. Protectively, she slid a hand around her baby. Mia couldn't fathom giving this baby away, even if it meant a better life for the child. Olivia's courage forty years ago astounded Mia, and she only hoped Bronson saw how his mother had always put her children's welfare first.

Because if Bronson didn't make peace with his mother and Anthony, there was no hope for her and the baby.

For the last hour Bronson had stared at his computer screen. Actually, at the title page of the script he and his mother had worked on, to be exact.

Everything had changed since they began working on writing their own film over a year ago. The script had been very loosely based on his mother's life in the movie industry. She'd been adamant about keeping her personal life from the script. At first he'd assumed it was simply because she wanted to keep their personal family life to herself.

Now he knew she didn't want to get into the fact that she'd given up her first child for adoption.

Bronson closed the script and came to his feet. His life had changed dramatically in the last three weeks, and he still hadn't figured out what steps to take next. Who the hell did he trust? Victoria had certainly taken the news better than he had, but Victoria had always had a heart of gold and gave everyone a chance. One of these days she was going to get her heart broken.

There was nowhere for him to direct his anger. The emotion seemed to shoot out in so many different directions. He wanted to hate his mother for keeping something like this from him, but at the same time he knew she lived her own hell by not being with a child she'd given birth to and then by seeing her two sons turn into rivals in the public eye.

As for his feelings for Anthony, Bronson honestly didn't know what to feel. Anger crept up from any emotion he battled with lately, but it wasn't Anthony's fault. He'd been given up for adoption and just recently discovered his mother was Hollywood's most beloved star. As much as Bronson hated to admit it, Anthony was a victim of fate, too.

But Mia, the woman who carried his child and claimed to love him, had known for months. In all that time, she'd worked her way into his life with that innocent smile and loving nature. She'd simply glowed whenever talking about the baby.

Bronson ran a hand through his hair, turning to look out the wide window behind his desk. And now he was back to doubting the baby's paternity. How could he trust her with anything? Did loyalty mean nothing to people anymore? How could he be so naive as to fall for another woman's lies?

Dammit. How many times had he lectured himself not to get too attached to another child? He'd known going in that Mia's past working relationship with Anthony made her questionable.

But he'd gone and fallen in love with the child anyway, and he knew, looking back, there was no way around it. The first time he'd seen the baby on the screen, the little heartbeat thump that resounded through the tiny exam room, there was no way anyone could avoid falling in love with that moment, that baby.

Bronson hated this helpless feeling that had plagued him since he'd come back from Italy and discovered the truth. Hated that control had been taken from his life and he'd had no way to stop it.

But he intended to get his life back in order, and the only

way he knew to start was to confront each of the key players: his mother, Anthony and Mia.

The war raged within him, but he knew the person he needed to start with was the one who'd had the shock of his life, too.

Bronson didn't call, didn't want to think about his plan. He ran down to the kitchen, grabbed the keys to his two-door sports car and headed toward Anthony's house before he could talk himself out of confronting him.

If Anthony wasn't home, then Bronson would go to his mother. But right now he was too angry, and he didn't want to talk to his mother when there was a good chance he'd say something he regretted. As far as offending Anthony, Bronson didn't care. There was no love lost there to begin with.

In less than twenty minutes Bronson arrived in front of Anthony's gated home. He pulled next to the guard's post and rolled down his window.

"Is Mr. Price in?"

The guard's eyes widened in recognition and he nodded. "Is Mr. Price expecting you, Mr. Dane?"

Bronson shook his head. "No, but if you tell him I'm here, I'm sure he'll see me."

The guard disappeared into the small post and within seconds the long, black wrought-iron gate slid open, allowing him access.

Bronson hadn't even come up with a course of action, but he had a feeling once he was in the same room with Anthony their conversation would take on a life of its own.

The palm-lined drive led Bronson to the light brick, three-story home—a place where Bronson had never envisioned himself.

Anthony stood in the doorway and something clenched in Bronson's gut as he stepped from his car. This man was his brother. There was no escaping the truth, no matter how much he wanted to. So now he had to deal with this information as best he could and not make this any more uncomfortable for his mother.

Besides, this would eventually leak to the press, and he wanted them all to appear as a united front. No need to make things more difficult on everyone.

"I wondered if you'd be by," Anthony said as Bronson approached. "Come on in."

Anthony led him into a formal sitting room just off the open foyer. Two large leather sofas faced each other for an intimate conversation setting, but Bronson hoped he wouldn't be here long enough to get that cozy. This was already way beyond his comfort zone, but he had to step outside the box if he wanted to get his life back on stable ground.

Anthony motioned to the wet bar in the corner. "Need a drink?"

"No, thanks."

Bronson took a seat on one of the sofas and leaned forward on his knees. "How did you find out?"

Taking a seat opposite him, Anthony sighed. "I've always known I was adopted. My parents were upfront about that from as far back as I can remember. But it wasn't until about a year and a half ago, when my own parents passed away, that I just wanted to know where I came from. Now that my adoptive parents are gone, it's just me and my sister. I didn't want to disrupt a family, but I wanted to know."

Bronson listened as Anthony poured out his past, his heart. A little bit of that hatred that had built up for years started to ebb. He'd come here ready for war, but seeing Anthony, listening to how much he wanted to find out where he came from, Bronson couldn't get angry. This

182

was just a man looking for some answers, and the answers happened to weave around Bronson's life.

"When my investigators came up with Olivia's name, I made them check again," Anthony went on. "I mean, I just didn't believe it. She'd done a very thorough job of keeping things under wraps."

Bronson's heart clenched. His mother had secretly watched over her son, and she'd shared that grief, that love, with no one but Bronson's father. When he died, she'd had no confidant at all.

"So why didn't you confront her months ago when you discovered the truth?"

Anthony's gaze faltered before coming back up to meet Bronson's. "It's no secret that my personal life is falling apart. My marriage is a disaster, and I was trying to get my feet under me before I approached Olivia. Unfortunately, that's not happening any time soon. I had to take back control in some part of my life. I wanted one-on-one time with her so we could decide where to go."

Damn. He hated the burst of jealousy that speared through him. Because of all the people on this earth, his sworn rival turned out to be the brother he never knew he had. And if Bronson were in Anthony's shoes, he'd be doing the exact same thing. Trying to regain control and determined to find some answers.

"And what did you two decide?"

Anthony shrugged. "Right now we're taking it one day at a time. Mostly phone calls, though, because we don't want the press to question why we're talking. Nobody needs that right now, with my marriage on the rocks, you and Mia expecting a baby."

Bronson sat straight up. "I wondered how long it would take you to weave Mia into the mix."

"There's no weaving her," Anthony said, eyes narrowing. "She's in it thanks to you."

"Me? I'm not the one who sent her to work for my biological mother all the while knowing about this secret."

Anthony shook his head. "No, you're the one who got her pregnant and probably broke her heart. Have you already confronted her about the fact that she knew?"

Bronson gritted his teeth. "What Mia and I discuss is none of your concern."

"She's too good for you," Anthony threw back. "I told her that when she told me who she was going to work for. I told her you'd try to sink your playboy claws into her, and I tried to warn her."

"And what were you warning her for? Because you wanted her for yourself? Because your wife wasn't enough—you had to get Mia, too?"

Anthony came to his feet. "I've never, *ever* cheated on my wife, and I'm damn sick of being accused of it. I love Mia like a sister, and I know these rumors are killing her, especially now that she's pregnant."

Bronson didn't know what to believe. A few weeks ago he did, but now…did the truth matter anymore? Another supposed "truth" would just come along later and void the previous one.

So what the hell was he supposed to do?

"I know your mind is turning a hundred miles an hour," Anthony went on. "And I know we've never gotten along, but I assure you I never, ever laid a hand on Mia in a personal, intimate way. She was like my assistant, best friend and sister all rolled into one and I hated to see her go. She chose to leave because of the strain the rumors were putting on my marriage. In my opinion, that's a hell of a woman to put others' needs first."

Bronson came to his feet and paced around the room. "It was Mia's idea to come work for my mother—not yours?"

"Mine?" Anthony laughed. "I begged her to stay. I never wanted to lose her."

Balls of tension built in Bronson's neck. He twisted it to the right, to the left, trying to relieve the pressure. God help him, he was starting to believe Anthony. Either he was a fool or he'd finally opened his eyes.

Bronson turned to face Anthony. "You've never cheated on your wife?"

"Never. Not with Mia, not with anyone."

"Not with Jennifer?"

Anthony jerked his head back. "Heavens, no. Why would you ask that?"

He was telling the truth. The stunned reaction, the shock in his tone told Bronson all he needed to know. Jennifer had played him.

"No reason."

No way did Anthony need to know what Bronson's ex-fiancée had accused him of. Which meant either she'd slept with someone else…or that baby had been his.

Dammit, why did his life keep circling back to lies and confusion, hurt and betrayal?

"I know there's no love lost between us," Anthony said, resting a hip on the edge of the sofa. "But whatever happens with Mia, be careful with her. She tries to be tough, but she's not. She has a tender heart and she truly has no one she can rely on."

Bronson ran a hand through his hair. "I won't talk about Mia's heart with you, Anthony."

"Fine, but know that she means a lot to me."

Bronson swallowed and nodded. She meant a lot to him,

too. Damn if he wasn't in the same scandalous situation he'd been in two years ago.

Except this time, his feelings for the woman were completely different.

Seventeen

Mia settled onto the exam table, more than ready to find out the sex of her baby. She'd hoped this would be a happy day, one with Bronson at her side, holding her hand while beaming at the screen. But that was not to be. She hadn't talked to him in the three weeks since he'd stormed out of her house, and she was not going to go to him. Once he had time to think, to process all this information, he could come to her. If he still wanted her.

Just as the ultrasound tech walked into the room, Bronson fell into step behind her and entered.

Relief surged through her. God, how she'd wanted him here, wanted him so bad she wondered if she didn't just wish him to appear.

"Am I late?" he asked, coming to stand beside the table.

The tech smiled. "Not at all. I'm just getting started."

Mia glanced up to Bronson. "I didn't think you'd come."

"I told you I'd be part of this baby's life."

She'd hoped Bronson was here out of his concern and love, not obligation. Had he changed his mind? Did he question her again about who the father was?

He didn't reach for her hand, didn't even look at her again as the tech moved the probe over her belly.

"There's the heart." The tech pointed on the screen. "All the arteries and vessels look good. Let's take some measurements so we can determine the approximate weight."

Mia watched, waiting with anticipation to make sure everything on her baby was healthy and normal. Nothing else mattered but the welfare of her child. Not Bronson's anger, not the secret she'd kept. Nothing.

"Your baby weighs about nine ounces and has a very healthy heart and organs." She adjusted the probe. "Now let's see if we can determine the sex."

Mia glanced back to Bronson, who kept his eyes on the screen. She might as well be here alone. He showed no sign of affection toward her, no brush of his hand against hers, no eye contact. The words he'd spoken were cold.

"Looks like we have a girl."

Mia's gaze jerked back to the screen. "A girl? Are you sure?"

The tech pointed to the screen. "Positive. The new imaging machines make this so easy to determine. See?"

Mia saw indeed. "Is she putting her toes in her mouth?"

The tech laughed. "She is. Most babies develop personalities in utero. Your little one is playful."

Just then the baby turned, exchanging toes for a thumb. Mia's eyes misted as she watched her baby's activity. A new life she and Bronson had created. How could he not want to reach out and touch her hand? Had he already distanced himself that much? Was he completely through with her?

"I've printed some pictures for you to take with you," the

tech said. "I'd like to do another ultrasound closer to thirty-
two weeks if you want to go ahead and get that scheduled.
Do either of you have any questions?"

Mia shook her head.

"No," Bronson answered, taking the photographs the
tech held out to him. "Thank you."

"I'll just step out and let you dress," she told Mia.

Mia climbed down from the table and started toward the
small bathroom off the exam room.

"Mia."

She turned, looking into the eyes of the man she feared
she'd always love, but could never have. "Yes?"

"I meant what I said. I'll be here for the baby."

"Just the baby, Bronson?" Mia clutched the paper-thin
gown to her chest, trying to keep the hurt from entering
her heart. "You may not want to admit it because you feel
I betrayed you, but you know I did nothing wrong. I understand you want to place blame somewhere, but don't use
me and this baby as your targets."

"How am I supposed to feel, Mia?" He stepped closer,
the muscle ticking in his jaw. "I've been lied to and ma-
nipulated in a situation just like this before."

Pulling all her courage to the surface, Mia swallowed
any fear and knew she needed to explain where she was
coming from. "I've already told you I was in the car when
my parents were killed. I overheard my mother on the
phone telling someone she was expecting a baby. I was so
excited, and I asked her about it. She said not to tell anyone,
but I didn't think she meant I couldn't tell my dad. I mentioned it in the car because I couldn't hold it in any longer.
They immediately started arguing. At the time I didn't
know what they were so upset about, but I remember my
father saying something about the baby not being his because he'd had surgery."

Mia leaned against the doorway to the bathroom, praying Bronson understood her actions, hoping he'd realize just how much she did love him.

"I replayed that conversation over and over in my head for years," she went on. "I still do. If I'd kept my mouth shut, kept my mother's secret, they'd still be alive. I vowed that day that I would never tell another secret. And I haven't. I love you, Bronson, but if you can't understand and forgive me for not sharing Anthony's secret with you, then I don't know if there can be a future for us."

Before he could say anything, Mia turned to the bathroom and shut the door. With shaky hands she dropped the gown into the laundry bin and redressed. She wanted to be with Bronson more than anything, but this battle he waged with himself could not be part of their relationship…if they had one left to salvage.

In her heart, Mia believed all was not lost and Bronson still cared. Somewhere beneath his rage and torment, he cared, more than likely even loved her. She had to believe, to hold on to that love because it was the single weapon she had to use to keep this family alive.

She smoothed her Victoria Dane custom-designed sundress over her rounded belly and opened the door. Bronson was nowhere to be found, and the pictures of the baby were lying on the counter near her purse.

Mia slid a finger over the picture of the baby's face and vowed to do everything in her power to keep this baby in a stable, loving home, no matter what the future held for her and Bronson.

She only hoped her plan to push him away long enough to think and allow him to sort out his feelings about his upturned life would pay off. For both her and their baby.

Bronson made a late-night trip to his mother's house. After seeing the baby on the ultrasound earlier in the day, he'd done nothing but think about his mother and the decision she'd made decades ago.

That's not true. He'd also thought of the hurt he'd seen in Mia's eyes. Bronson knew there was nothing more she wanted than her own family, but he wasn't here to be part of a fairy tale. This wasn't a script, this was his life, and he honestly had no clue what the ending would be.

He found his mother sitting in the formal living room, reading. The timeless Hollywood icon sat with her legs folded beneath her on a white chaise. An oil painting of a young Olivia holding her first Oscar hung on the wall opposite the doorway. His eyes traveled from the portrait to the woman, a smile spread across his face. Not much had changed. His mother had truly grown more graceful with the years.

"Mom."

Startled, Olivia jerked her head toward the door. "My heavens, you scared me." She set her book, open side down, over her leg. "I've been waiting for you to come back once you had time to think."

Bronson moved into the room, too restless to sit, too exhausted to pace. There was no happy place for him lately—except when he'd seen the baby on the screen.

"We're having a girl," he blurted out.

Olivia clasped her hands together. "Oh, how wonderful, Bronson. I'm so glad you and Mia patched things up. Is she excited?"

Bronson walked to the wet bar, tempted to get a drink, but knowing no alcohol could change his fate. He leaned an elbow against the dark wood bar.

"We haven't patched things up," he informed her. "I went to the appointment and left after I found out the sex and that the baby was healthy. I promised Mia I would be there for the baby."

Olivia moved her book to the coffee table and swung her legs down. "Just the baby? Mia doesn't warrant the same devotion?"

Bronson shrugged. "I'm not quite ready to take Mia at face value, considering the circumstances."

"Oh, son. You know in your heart she was in a rough position. Why torture yourself and Mia? She's just as torn up about this as you are. I guarantee she battled with herself over whether to tell you because I can assure you, that woman loves you with every ounce of her being."

Bronson raked a hand through his hair. He didn't want to hear about Mia's loyalty or love for him when she also had loyalties to Anthony. Besides, love was based on trust. Plain and simple. And he'd finally begun to trust her before this latest life-altering blow.

"I'm here to talk about you," he told her. "Mia can take care of herself."

Olivia's eyes closed. "If you truly think that, then you don't know the girl at all."

He couldn't get into this. He was still trying to come to grips with everything and sort through his feelings. Couldn't people understand that he couldn't take another betrayal?

"When I saw the baby on the screen today, I thought of you." Bronson pushed off the bar and moved across the wide room to sit in a wing-back chair across from his mother. "How you must've felt to give up a child, how selfless the act was."

"The act was utterly selfish, Bronson. I gave Anthony up because I was starting a promising career and was rising fast in the movie industry. I knew I wanted a career first and a family later, and I wasn't even in love. I had a fling—plain and simple. I was a selfish woman."

"That's not selfish, Mom, that's love."

Olivia batted a hand in the air. "Maybe so, but I knew giving him to a family who wanted a child would be best. Soon after, Anthony's parents discovered they were going to have a baby of their own. Giving him up was the hardest decision of my life, and I questioned myself every day, but I know, looking back, I did what was right."

Bronson leaned forward on his knees. "Tell me the truth. Did you not tell me and Victoria because you thought we'd be disappointed or because Anthony and I are rivals and you were afraid of the outcome?"

With misty eyes, Olivia smiled. "Both. I was afraid if you found out Anthony was your half brother, you'd hate him more. But mostly I feared you and your sister would look at me with disappointment in your eyes. I worried what you'd think of me."

Bronson's heart melted. "I think you're human. Do I like that you kept this from us? No. Do I like that Anthony is a blood relation? Hell, no. But I love you, Mom. Unconditionally and forever."

A cry escaped Olivia as she closed her eyes against the tears. "You don't know how much I wanted you to feel that way, to understand my actions and not hate me."

Bronson moved to sit next to his mother. Wrapping an arm around her, he pulled her to his side. "When I saw that baby today I realized that I would do anything to ensure a good, stable life for her. That's when I realized you had to have battled this guilt for years. All you wanted was to give Anthony a good life with a loving family."

Except for when his father died of a sudden heart attack, Bronson had never seen his mother this vulnerable, this emotional.

"Please, Bronson," his mother sniffed. "Please don't throw away what you have with Mia. Try to make this work. She loves you and she loves this baby."

"How can I be sure she won't deceive me?"

Olivia sat up, looked him in the eye. "If she were out to deceive you or she had something going on with Anthony, don't you think she would've gone to the tabloids the second she uncovered the truth?"

Bronson swallowed. "I suppose. I just can't live with another broken heart."

"Who says you have to?" Olivia patted her damp cheeks. "I can almost guarantee that if you go to Mia, she'll not only welcome you with open arms, she'll forgive you for doubting her. That's how true love works. It's forgiving. You've forgiven me, haven't you?"

Bronson smiled. "There's nothing to forgive."

"And that's how Mia will feel. Don't shut her out when you need each other most. Believe me—love only comes once. Don't waste time arguing over my past sins."

Pulling his mother into another hug, Bronson kissed her cheek. "Quit blaming yourself for this. All your children turned out fine. We all love you and we're going to be okay. Somehow, this will all work out."

"What do we tell the media?" Olivia asked, fear lacing her voice.

"Nothing." He pulled back. "We wait until we are comfortable talking about this, until we all can stand before a camera as a united front."

Her eyes bore into his. "Can you do that? Can you bury your hatred for Anthony?"

Bronson swallowed. "I'm beginning to realize he's not the man I thought he was. True, we clash on film sets, but as for the private life he's led, it's not nearly as wild and deceitful as I'd thought."

"So you'll make this work?"

The hope in Olivia's eyes, in her voice had Bronson nodding. "But first I have to get my own life straightened out."

He kissed his mother one last time on the cheek. He might have a great deal of groveling in his immediate future, but the end result with Mia and his baby in his life was all that mattered at this point.

Eighteen

Nearly six months along in the pregnancy and Mia had never felt better. Other than her disappearing waist, she had no complaints. But every time she felt a kick or a swift movement from her baby girl, the waistline was all but forgotten and joy filled her.

The baby name book wasn't giving her any suggestions she thought she—or the baby—could live with for the rest of her life. She'd been through the thing at least five times and nothing resonated with her.

Of course, her heart hadn't really been in the search because this was not something she wanted to decide on her own. She wanted Bronson at her side, giving suggestions, laughing when she chose silly name combinations.

But since she'd seen him in the doctor's office yesterday, he'd only called to double-check on her next exam appointment. Other than that, he'd said nothing on a more personal level.

And there was only so long she would wait before she marched to his mansion and made him see what he was throwing away because of pride and fear. She'd tossed down the proverbial gauntlet, so why hadn't he picked it up?

Why did men let such negative emotions rule their love lives? And speaking of negative emotions, Mia was still reeling from Anthony's phone call earlier when he'd told her that he and Charlotte had separated. But she couldn't dwell on that now.

Mia glanced at the boxes sitting in the room she'd had painted a very pale pink. The furniture had arrived yesterday, and she'd instructed the deliveryman to put everything in here. The bedding would arrive shortly if Bronson called Fabrizio to tell him the baby's gender.

When she and Bronson had ordered the crib and bedding, she certainly hadn't expected to be the only one putting it all together. She'd envisioned them working as a team, taking an occasional break to feel the baby moving within her belly, sharing a smile of recognition that they were going to be parents in just a few short months.

Mia moved into the room. There was no way she could move anything by herself. Maybe some of Olivia's staff would come help.

Mia tore into the boxes and smiled. The circular crib was going to look perfect tucked into the corner between the windows. Trailing a finger along the edge, Mia couldn't wait to see her baby all snuggled up, safe in her bed with the chandelier-type mobile hanging overhead.

She moved to the smaller boxes and opened them, curious to know what else there might be. The second her eyes landed on the pale-pink-and-ivory bumper cover, Mia's breath caught. The soft swirl pattern was so much more delicate and precious than she'd hoped.

As her finger slid over the ruffled edge, tears clogged her throat. This was supposed to be a joyous time, a moment every woman would remember.

She looked deeper into the box to find her boy bedding. A note attached to the bumper read, "Send back what you don't need...or keep for the next *bambino*. Love, F."

For a second, Mia closed her eyes, giving in to the tears. She was so happy for this baby to come into her life and didn't regret a moment of being with Bronson. She just wished she hadn't allowed herself to open her heart so freely when she knew she was going to get hurt. She'd known from the start that she carried a secret that would change his life. How could she blame him for being so angry and not believing anything she said now?

On a sigh, Mia wiped her damp cheeks. "I can do this on my own. I'm stronger than I think."

"Yes, you are."

Mia spun around to see Bronson standing in the doorway of the nursery. "What are you doing here?"

Casual as you please, he lifted a shoulder, but kept those mesmerizing eyes focused directly on her. "I wasn't sure if I'd be welcome, so I let myself in since I knew your code."

With slow, easy steps, he crossed the room to stand directly in front of her. Mia tipped her head back to look up into those eyes she'd so easily fallen in love with.

Bronson slid a thumb over her cheek, wiping away one lone tear. "Are those tears over me, sweet Mia?"

The words may have sounded cocky if he hadn't delivered them with such agony in his own tone, such torment in his eyes.

Mia blinked and cleared her throat. "My tears are over a lot lately."

His eyes roamed over her face and she just knew she looked like a mess. At this point, though, what did it matter? She was turning into a whale. But, God, she'd waited for him to come to her. Waited and prayed.

"You're not sleeping well," he told her, running a fingertip below her eyes. "I'm sorry."

Mia jerked away, shocked those two words came from his mouth. "What are you sorry for?"

She turned back to the boxes, unable to be so close to him.

"Everything," he whispered in her ear as his hands came to cup her shoulders, pulling her back against his chest. "I'm sorry for everything. For denying this child is mine, for not being the man you needed me to be, but most of all for not returning the precious gift you so freely offered me."

Mia's head dropped to her chest. So much for holding those tears back. "And what gift was that?"

Bronson turned her around, lifting her chin with his fingertip. "Love. Your unconditional gift of love was so rare to me. I didn't believe it, didn't believe in you or us."

Hope speared through her, but fear accompanied it. Could she allow herself to let her guard down again? Bronson wouldn't be here if he didn't believe her and, dare she hope, love her.

"I know what I did may not have been the right decision, but Bronson, it wasn't my place to say."

"I realize that now." He kissed the top of her head. "If I'd been in your shoes, I can't say what I would've done, but I know that what you did was right. There aren't many people who make the right decision when they're under pressure. I was so angry I wasn't sure if I could forgive you."

Bronson stared back at her, then reached to pull her into his strong, warm embrace. Mia fell against his chest and sighed.

"And now?" she dared to ask, tipping her head back to look into his eyes.

"Now I've fallen in love with a woman who only eats green M&M's, who has persevered through life no matter what the odds and who I want to spend the rest of my life with so she can try amazing new recipes in my gourmet kitchen. I want to spend the rest of my life showing you how much you mean to me, how much your loyalty and integrity have made me a better person." He swiped a lone tear that trickled down her cheek. "I want to wake up every morning and see you next to me. I want to make more children with you so we have a house full of love that can come only from the bond we have. But most of all, I want you to know that I was a fool for ever doubting you. Let me spend the next fifty years showing you how much I love you."

Mia's breath caught. "Is that a proposal?"

Bronson stepped back, reached into his pocket and held out a locket. "It's not to replace the one you have, but I thought you might want a picture of your new family to keep with you."

"Oh, God."

Bronson smiled. "How am I doing in making up for being a jerk? Because I'll grovel more, Mia. I'll do anything to make you see just how serious I am about loving you and committing myself to our family."

"Our family," she repeated.

His image blurred as her eyes collected with more tears than she could hold. They fell down her cheek, one after another, as a laugh escaped her. "You're amazing. The locket is… God, Bronson, I don't know what to say."

Bronson slid the chain around her neck and fastened it, then pulled a small box from his pocket.

"Just how much do you have in those pockets for me?" she joked through tears.

"Not nearly enough to make up for my actions," he told her, opening the velvet box. "This is the ring my father gave my mother."

"What? Bronson, I can't take her ring."

"When I told her my plans, she insisted. This isn't her original engagement ring—that one she'll never part with. He gave her this on the night I was born for this purpose right here. To pass down to the woman I will marry." He took her hand, sliding the ring on. "Perfect fit."

Mia eyed the ring on her finger. The glistening diamonds stole her breath, but had someone else worn this before?

"No," he said, as if reading her thoughts. "I didn't give this to my ex-fiancée. She wanted a new ring, and when she asked to go ring shopping, I didn't even mention that I had this. I should've known then she wasn't the one."

Unable to contain her excitement one more second, Mia threw her arms around Bronson's neck, but their baby stopped her from getting too close.

"Oh, sorry." She laughed. "Bella is growing pretty fast these days."

Bronson raised a brow. "Bella?"

"Um, I call her that. It means—"

"Beautiful," he whispered before capturing her lips for a brief kiss. "Just like her mother."

His kiss never failed to send a jolt of love and hope through her.

"Let's start our life together," he murmured against her lips.

Epilogue

"Are you ever going to put her down?"

With a radiant smile on her face, Bronson's wife of two months rocked their sleeping daughter. A sight he never tired of seeing.

"She's just so sweet," Mia whispered. "I could look at her all day."

Bronson knew exactly how she felt. He eased off the door frame and crept into the room, loving the look of his family—Bella, with her mother's dark wispy hair and almond-shaped chocolate eyes, and Mia with her glow that never ceased to clutch his heart.

He knelt down beside the plush rocker they'd ordered on their trip to Italy. "You're going to have to let her sleep on her own, you know."

Mia's lips brushed the top of Bella's head. "I know. I just want her to know how much she's loved."

"I'm sure she knows." Bronson wrapped an arm around

Mia, leaned his head against hers and watched his child sleep, nestled against Mia's chest. "I love you, Mia. Love you more every day."

"I love you, too."

"I just hung up with Anthony."

"Bella's a heavy sleeper. Tell me." Mia's rocking slowed. "Did you ask him to work with you on your mother's film?"

"We've talked about it. We're taking this one day at a time. We know how important this is to Mom, and we can't let our past differences affect the movie. We both want this to be the best film either of us have ever produced and directed."

Mia adjusted the white blanket over Bella's tiny hands. "I think that says a lot about where the two of you are now in your journey."

"Yeah, it does." Bronson cleared his throat. "I want him to help me produce it, not just direct."

Mia's misty gaze came up to meet his. "Oh, Bronson. That's wonderful."

Bronson's heart clenched at the sight of his wife, his daughter and this talk of producing a movie with his half brother. "I haven't asked him, but I plan on it."

"I'm so happy for the two of you."

Bronson kissed the tip of her nose. "I'm happy for me, too. I never imagined I could have everything I ever wanted, but I do."

Mia's smile lit her up from within. "Trust me, I know all about dreams coming true."

* * * * *

BILLIONAIRE'S BABY
Leanne Banks

One

"That's mine!" a voice echoing with feminine distress called out, making Garrett lift his head from the waters of Chankanaab Park in Cozumel. An orange bathing suit top floated to his side in the turquoise waters.

Garrett had taken a day to snorkel, and he'd expected to see plenty of tropical fish, but not this. A parrot fish nudged the orange triangles to check for edibility, then swam away.

"Could you—please!"

Garrett turned his head to catch sight of a young woman with strawberry-blond hair slicked back from her forehead, her mask on top of her head and her eyes wide with embarrassment.

The parrot fish was dead wrong. This woman was definitely edible.

"The current carried it away," she said, crossing her arms over her chest. "If you could just send it over here..."

"I don't know. Haven't you heard? Finders keepers," he said, unable to resist the urge to tease her just a little.

Kicking her fins to keep herself afloat, she gave a long-suffering sigh. "Aw, c'mon. Orange isn't your color."

"Maybe not," he mused thoughtfully as he held the top out of the water. Looked like the cups would take just a little bit more than a mouthful. "What's the reward for the top?" he asked, looking at her again.

She lifted her chin. "A gentleman wouldn't ask for a reward."

"I never said I was a gentleman. On the flip side, a lady would give a token of her gratitude."

"What'd you have in mind?"

"Dinner tonight," he said, meeting her gaze dead-on.

"If you can deliver the top of that bathing suit and keep your eyes on my eyes—with no detours lower," she emphasized, "I'll meet you for dinner in town."

"Deal," he said, though he knew the effort would cost him. He wouldn't be a man if he didn't want to see her naked, and the clear water would have made the viewing oh, so easy.

"Since you've already said you're not much of a gentleman, I imagine I'll be eating dinner with my friends," she said in a cool voice, keeping her eyes trained on his as she moved closer. He made damn sure his gaze never wavered, never dipped. He had an odd feeling in his gut about this woman.

His eyes fastened on hers, he pressed the suit top into her outstretched hand.

"Thanks," she said, surprise shimmering in her gaze.

"Turn around," he told her, his voice a little rough around the edges.

She did, then fidgeted with the clasp. She made a sound of frustration. "I can't make it stay."

"Wait a minute. I've got a rubber band on my wrist," he told her, treading closer. "You want me to try it?"

"Please."

Garrett made a makeshift fastener and looped the two ends of the suit together. He gave it a slight tug. "Okay?"

She nodded and turned around. "Thanks. Really." She paused then, as if on impulse, she leaned toward him and brushed her lips over his. "A token of gratitude," she said.

Garrett licked the combination of salty sweetness from his lips and felt a slow burn. "Alberto's at seven. What's your name and where are you staying?"

"Haley. Haley Turner. I'm at Plaza Las Glorias. And you are?"

He opened his mouth to tell her his name, but thought better of it. The temptation to give in to the freedom of anonymity was too much. He'd been burned so many times by women who had wanted him for his family name, money or both. He'd always wanted to know if a woman could want him for himself instead of all the trappings associated with being a Winslow.

He felt a twinge of conscience but pushed it aside. If things worked out, he would tell her the truth later. "Rick Williams," he said.

Four days later, he was totally entranced. While the sun set in downtown Cozumel, Garrett Winslow watched Haley snap a photo of two Mexican children selling marionettes on the busy street corner. The children smiled for Haley.

From what Garrett had observed, everyone smiled for Haley. With her strawberry-blond hair and easy laugh, she had an unpretentious air that was like pure oxygen for Garrett. He couldn't get enough of her. At odd moments, he envisioned their relationship extending past their time in Cozumel.

She made him feel content and ravenous for her at the same time. He had wanted her in his bed since the first minute he'd seen her. Maybe by the end of the night, he thought. He could feel the crackle of expectancy sizzling between them. He wanted to tell her his real name, but the delicious appeal of attracting her purely on a personal basis stopped him.

Within months, he would take on the role for which he'd been born and bred. Vice-president-in-training for Winslow Corporation, the company his father, grandfather and great-grandfather had built and nurtured.

He would graduate from law school in weeks. His roommate had persuaded him to go to Mexico for spring break for one last hurrah. And what a hurrah, he thought, mesmerized by the sway of Haley's hips beneath the skirt that skimmed just above the knee to reveal long shapely legs.

She glanced around at him and, with a grin, shook her head. She waggled her finger. "You're staring again."

"You've got a lot worth staring at," he told her, catching her hand in his and dragging her against him for a quick kiss.

Her slightly sunburned cheeks turned even pinker, but she didn't stiffen or pull back as she had the first couple of days he'd cajoled her into spending time with him. "Are you trying to take my breath away?"

"Turnabout's fair play," he said, staring into her green eyes.

Her gaze deepened with a sliver of doubt. "Bet you say that to all the girls at Yale."

"Don't bet the farm," he told her, unable to resist skimming his finger down a strand of her red-gold hair.

"What's so different about me, other than the fact that I lost my bathing suit top in the ocean and you rescued it for me?" she asked with a catch of laughter in her throat.

"You're real."

Haley felt her stomach flip at the look in Rick's eyes. Ever since the first time they'd met, she'd been intrigued by him. She'd been cautious at first, but now she was very curious and very attracted.

Haley was a good, sensible girl who attended a women's college on scholarship in Texas, but she didn't feel at all sensible when she was with Rick. She felt beautiful, interesting and sexy. He made her heart go pitter-patter, and all kinds of other places buzz.

She took a quick breath and tried to cling to sanity. Mexico was no place for a girl to lose her head. "Everyone's real."

He shook his head. "Not like you. I want to dance with you tonight."

"Carlos 'n' Charlie's?" she asked. The wild, rowdy bar was the most popular spot with the spring break crowd.

He shook his head. "Too loud."

"Then where?"

"A store owner told me about a place that plays blues and jazz."

"Sounds nice," she said, feeling a reckless anticipation bubbling inside her.

Two hours later, after a dinner of fajitas and two margaritas, she was swaying to sultry music in Rick's arms. She probably shouldn't have had that second margarita, but Haley felt as if she'd been sensible her entire life. She wanted to cut loose and enjoy herself for once.

She stumbled slightly, and Rick drew her body flush against his.

"Sorry," she said, breathless. "A little dizzy."

"After just two margaritas?" he gently teased.

"It doesn't take much for me, but I don't think it's just

the tequila." She looked into his eyes and felt her stomach dip and sway.

"Then what is it?"

The alcohol loosened her tongue. "You."

He lowered his lips to her ear. "I don't believe you. You've been hard-to-get since we first met."

She shook her head. "There's a difference between hard-to-get and shy. And careful." She searched his face. She had felt the oddest, strangest connection with him right from the start.

His dark eyes darkened further with arousal and he lowered his mouth to hers, taking her lips in a French kiss that made the room spin. He slid his leg between hers, and she felt the hard evidence of his desire against her. She instinctively moved against him, and he groaned.

"You're going to drive me totally crazy, aren't you?" he muttered against her lips.

Her heart pounding a mile a minute, she shook her head. "Not me. I don't have that kind of power."

"You greatly underestimate yourself," he said in a wry voice and pulled back with a sigh. "I need some air. Let's go for a walk on the beach."

They left the sexy sounds of the jazz club and grabbed a cab to his hotel, which boasted the most walkable portion of the beach. That didn't say much, considering much of Cozumel's beach was rocky. They arrived at a good time, however, and ended up walking the narrow strip of sand several times.

"It's very strange," she said, allowing him to tug her down beside him on the beach. "I feel like I know you and don't know you at all."

He shrugged. "There's not much to know. I'm a simple guy."

"Liar," she said, playfully tossing a handful of sand on

his leg. She wasn't an idiot. She could tell he was a complicated man. He'd let her see parts of him, but she was convinced he kept some parts secret. The more she knew about him, the more she wanted to know.

He chuckled. "Okay. What do you want to know?"

"That's easy. What do you want more than anything?"

His gaze grew serious, and he laced his fingers between hers. "Right now? Right this very minute?"

Two

Haley couldn't have breathed if her life had depended on it. She bit her lip at the rush of emotions that rolled through her. She forced herself to look away from Rick's dark gaze to regain her equilibrium. "Before you came to Mexico, what did you want?"

He lifted her hand to his lips, and she closed her eyes at the tenderness in the gesture. "To meet a woman like you."

It should have sounded like a line, but it didn't. And the same feeling resonated inside her. She had always wanted to meet a man like Rick. Fun but intelligent. Sexy, with heart.

"Hey, what happened?" he asked, his hand touching her foot.

Haley glanced down and saw a trickle of bright red blood on her toe. "I must've stepped on something, maybe a rock." She shrugged. "It doesn't hurt. It's no big deal."

"Band-Aid and antibiotic ointment," he said firmly, pulling her to her feet.

"There's no need to make a fuss," she protested.

"If you end up with an infection, you'll really be fussing. C'mon. I've got the supplies in my room. It won't take but a minute."

As they took the elevator to his room, in some corner of her mind, it occurred to Haley that it might not be prudent to be anywhere near a bed with Rick. The temptation to do more and go further had been simmering between them for days, and tonight it was stronger than ever. But she knew Rick wouldn't force her into anything. This was just a first-aid mission, not a seduction scene.

He motioned her toward the sofa as soon as he unlocked the door, then flicked on a light and opened the door to the balcony before he disappeared into the adjoining bedroom. He returned with a washcloth, a tube of ointment and an adhesive bandage. Haley extended her hand to take the supplies from him.

He shook his head. "I'll do it."

"I can put on my own Band-Aid."

"Don't deprive me of a legitimate reason to touch your feet."

She smiled as he cleaned the sand from her foot. "You don't have a foot fetish, do you?"

"No, but you have very cute feet."

She curled her toes. "They're long."

"Like your legs," he said, his voice laced with rough approval.

"I always thought I was too skinny in high school."

Wrapping the toe in a bandage, he gave her body an appreciative glance. "Baby, you have filled out very well."

He made her feel as if she'd kept her nose stuck in the books entirely too long. What had she missed by focusing almost exclusively on her studies? Her college buddies had insisted she take this trip to Mexico for some fun, to hook up with a guy and be spontaneous for once. Everyone close to her knew she worked hard to keep her grades up so her scholarship wouldn't be threatened.

She was the first in her family to get a college education, and she never forgot how lucky she was to get to study photojournalism. She hadn't allowed herself to get distracted. She couldn't, but something inside her was pushing her toward Rick. The push was so strong it felt like a storm surge. Haley didn't know whether to fight it or let it take her....

"Thanks for the complimentary medical treatment," she said with a smile that she hoped covered her mixed emotions. "Are you sure you're not a med student?"

Chuckling, he helped her to her feet. "No chance of that. Take a look from the balcony. It's a nice view even at night."

Following him out to the balcony, she drew in a breath mixed with sea air and the subtle scent of his aftershave and looked at the reflection of the stars on the ocean. "It looks like magic."

He looked back at her. "Magic," he echoed. "I don't think it's the ocean. I think it's you." He dipped his head and took her mouth in a kiss that made her feel things she'd never felt—heat and need so intense she trembled with it.

He pulled back slightly. "You're shaking. Are you cold?"

"No," she said, swallowing over the lump in her throat. "I don't want this time with you to end."

He nodded slowly and slid his hands through her hair. "I feel the same way. I can't get close enough to you."

In the warm, strong circle of his arms, she felt the heavy beat of his heart and the urgent evidence of his need pressed against her. Her own need surged inside her, overriding years of good sense and restraint. She had never felt like this about a man before. She didn't want to miss him, to miss being with him. Something inside her broke free and she arched against him.

"How close do you want to be?" she whispered.

Time stopped between them, and Haley had the odd sensation of being in the eye of a hurricane.

Rick slid his hand to the small of her back to guide her more intimately against him. "As close as we can get," he murmured, then took her mouth again.

Heat roared through her. She loved the taste of him, and he touched her as if he knew exactly what would take her breath away and make her heart pound. She felt the strings of her sundress slip to her shoulders. Rick's mouth traveled down her throat to her chest, then he took her nipple into his warm, avid mouth.

A delicious combination of shock and desire coursed through her. She didn't have time to react before he skimmed one of his hands up her leg to her panties. She could have stopped him. If she'd wanted to stop him.

His fingers slid into her secret, damp swollen place, and he groaned. "I want all of you, Haley."

Her heart hammered in her throat. She knew she was at the point of no return. "I don't have any—" She swallowed. "I don't have any protect—"

He cut her off with one finger pressed to her lips. "I'll take care of you."

And she knew by the look in his eyes that he would. In every way a man can intimately care for the woman he wants. She closed her eyes for a second, scared, yet full of wanting, then opened them and met his gaze. "I want you."

His eyes lit with dark fire, and he took her mouth, took her body and took her heart. He made love to her with fierce gentleness, seducing her response. He kissed her mouth and throat, caressed her breasts to turgid points of desire. Then lower still, he pressed his open mouth to her belly and thighs, then between her thighs.

When he thrust inside her, she felt the melding of minds, bodies, souls. Even afterward, she clung to him, shaken by the power of their joining. As if he couldn't get enough of her, he made love to her again and again…. They finally slept wrapped in each other's arms.

Hours later, the jarring ringing of the phone abruptly awakened Haley. She sat bolt upright in bed, disoriented by her unfamiliar surroundings.

"Yes, yes, it's me," Rick said, sliding to sit on the edge of the bed. He stopped mid-movement. "Oh, my God! How bad is he?"

Haley's stomach clenched at the shock in his voice. She glanced at the alarm clock and bit her lip. Good news never came at two a.m.

"The jet's already on the way? I'll go to the airport right away." Rick paused. "If he regains consciousness, tell him I love him and I'm coming." He hung up the phone, his body taut with desperation. He took a deep breath then shook his head as if to clear it.

"What is it?" Haley asked.

Standing, Rick looked at her. "I have to leave. It's my father. He's had a heart attack."

Her heart ached for him. "That's terrible!"

He nodded, pulling out dresser drawers and throwing clothes into a suitcase. "I always thought he was as strong as an ox. I never thought he would—" He broke off, his voice catching.

She wrapped the sheet around herself and rushed to put her arms around him. "I'm really sorry. What can I do?"

Distracted and rightfully so, he shook his head. "Nothing. I just really need to go. I'm sorry. I'll be in touch with you. Okay?"

Haley tamped down a flood of insecurities. Now wasn't the time for her to ask for reassurance or declarations. "Okay," she made herself say. "I hope he'll be okay."

Ten minutes later, she watched him walk out the door and hoped with all her heart that it wasn't the last time she would see him.

Three

Four years later...

"It's nice of them to let us see the executioner before they send us to the guillotine," Susan Cooper said to Haley as the two of them walked toward the outdoor company courtyard to meet the new owner.

"Do you have to call him the executioner?" Haley asked, fighting her own nerves about the prospect of losing her job.

Susan Cooper shrugged. "That's how Garrett Winslow operates. He buys and takes over little companies like ours, then cuts away the fat, so to speak—" she glanced down at her plump abdomen and sucked it in "—of the employee workforce." She tossed Haley a mock scowl. "You don't have to worry. You're superslim."

"I'm in advertising. That can be farmed out or taken over by one of his other companies."

"But you take great photos and write great copy," Susan protested.

"I appreciate your loyalty, but I take photographs of computer components. I'm replaceable." Her stomach twisted with nerves. "I really don't want to lose this job. The day-care center is right across the street. I can visit Jake just about every day for lunch, and if there's a problem I can be there in less than two minutes."

Susan patted her shoulder in sympathy. "You'll be fine whatever happens. You've got your degree. You've got a great kid. And if you'll just cooperate, I could get you ten marriage proposals in no time."

Susan had been the best friend Haley could ever have since moving to Tremont, Texas, two years ago. A mother of two, married for fifteen years to a terrific husband, Susan worked as the assistant in Haley's department and had opened her heart and home to Haley and Jake right from the start.

"I don't need a husband. I just need things to stay the same," Haley said.

"Hmm. Well, I can guarantee that won't happen. C'mon, let's get a look at the executioner. He may hand us our pink slips, but I hear he's a hunk. He's a bachelor," she added with emphasis, then sighed. "But I also heard he has a beautiful blonde assistant who's angling for another position and making some progress in that direction."

Haley couldn't help smiling at Susan's ability to get the personal scoop on the new owner. "How do you get all this info?"

"I keep my ear to the ground and my nose to the wind."

"Sounds like a recipe for a crick in the neck."

"Aren't you cute?" Susan said with a chuckle.

"That's what you keep saying," Haley playfully retorted

as they approached the double glass doors, which led to the courtyard. "You go first."

"Age before beauty," Susan said with a sniff, then walked outside.

Haley's stomach twisted and turned as she hung near the back of the large crowd of employees of E-Z Computer Corporation. She wondered if the company would keep its name or become Winslow Computers. That would really mess up the marketing plans.

Her mind turned to her son, Jake. She wondered how he would adjust to a move if she lost her job. She feared the transition could be difficult. She had chosen the job at E-Z Computers because the management had offered flexibility, a great health benefits package, reasonable job security and Tremont, Texas, was the perfect place to raise a son. Now it appeared that her job security would be threatened.

Hearing a flurry of activity behind her, she moved to the side as a small entourage of people walked through the doorway. Haley identified the president and vice president of E-Z Computers, a beautiful blonde woman she pegged as Winslow's assistant and a tall, dark, handsome man who looked entirely familiar.

Her heart stopped. It was Rick Williams. The father of her child.

Garrett Winslow climbed the steps to the small platform as the president of E-Z Computers introduced him. Looking out over the crowd, he saw a mixture of curiosity and apprehension on the faces of the employees.

Both were understandable. In the past five years, Winslow Corporation had gained a reputation of taking over companies and making them lean and mean. After his father's death, Garrett had been thrown into a battle to keep the control of the company in a Winslow's hands. He'd had to prove himself by showing healthy profits from the word go.

He had succeeded and won the respect of every member on the board. If he'd sacrificed his personal life, then that was just a necessary loss. Maybe someday he would be able to have a life and family outside the confines of Winslow Corporation. But not now.

The employees applauded, signaling him to step up to the microphone.

"Good afternoon. Thank you for coming. I can't tell you how excited Winslow Corporation is to bring E-Z Computers into our family. E-Z has produced a superior product and marketed it in a highly inventive and effective fashion. We want to take E-Z to the next level." He automatically scanned the crowd as he spoke, and his gaze hung on the way the sun glinted on a woman's strawberry-blond hair in the back of the crowd.

He paused. His heart hesitated. His mind traveled backward, to what now seemed eons ago, to a time when his life had been simpler. A sweet time when he hadn't shouldered the burden of his father's death and his subsequent struggle to take the reins of Winslow. A time when a woman had wanted him just for him, and not the Winslow name and fortune.

He blinked. It couldn't be her. In lonely moments, he'd thought of her but never called. When his father had died on his return to the States, Garrett's life had changed in an instant. There'd been no time for dancing and laughing. There'd been no time for love.

He remembered the bitter guilt he'd felt. While he'd been playing in Cozumel, his father had been dying. Even though, logically, he'd known he couldn't have prevented his father's death, he'd punished himself by turning away from thoughts of Haley and drowning himself in work.

As time passed, however, he knew he'd let something precious slip away, and losing Haley had become his greatest regret.

He continued speaking, but his gaze returned to the woman in the back of the crowd. She flipped her hair behind her shoulder, and he got an odd feeling in his gut. If he could look into her eyes, he would know.

He wrapped up his speech and nodded at the applause, then turned to Bob Stevens, E-Z's president. "Bob, do you know if you have an employee by the name of Haley—"

"Haley Turner," Bob said with a broad smile. "Great employee. She's a great photographer, works in advertising. Everybody loves her."

"I often like to talk with a few of the employees during these visits. I'd like you to put her on the list for this afternoon." Garrett felt his pulse race but tried to remain outwardly calm. He wondered if he would find the words to explain. He wondered how she would respond to him. He wondered if there was a remote possibility that he could have her in his life again.

Four

"Mr. Winslow wants to see you." The words echoed inside Haley's brain as she walked down the hall to see Garrett Winslow. Her heart pounded a mile a minute. Had he recognized her? Was he going to fire her personally? Why her? Why not someone else? Of all the ways she'd fantasized seeing Rick again…Garrett, she mentally corrected. Of all the ways she'd fantasized Garrett coming into her life again, this hadn't been one of them. Taking a shaky breath, she opened the door to face her past.

The sight of her made Garrett's heart stop. Haley's face was pale, her eyes didn't quite meet his, and when he reached to take her hand, she hesitated then briefly pressed her cold palm against his.

"Take a seat, Haley," he said, leaning back against the desk.

"Mr. Winslow," she said with a short nod.

If he hadn't noticed her pale complexion and slight jit-
teriness, then he almost would believe that she'd forgotten
him. His gut twisted at the notion, but that was what he
deserved. "You like it here at E-Z Computers?"

"Yes, I do. I've enjoyed the family atmosphere of the
company. I hope that won't get lost in the transition."

"Family atmosphere is fine as long as it doesn't hold the
company back. Change is necessary to get ahead."

"That would be your area of expertise. Getting ahead,"
she said in a neutral tone.

She still didn't quite look at him, and that bothered the
hell out of him. He missed her warmth. He had missed it
for years, but now standing in front of her as she sealed
herself off from him like a cold vault, he missed it even
more. "You're afraid of losing your job?"

"Of course. Everyone is," she said, lacing her fingers
together. He could almost remember how her hands had
felt on him. "Your reputation precedes you."

He narrowed his eyes at her words. "What do you mean
'my reputation'?"

She hesitated, emanating discomfort. "Just some talk
I've heard."

"I'd like to know what the talk is."

"I'm not sure you really want to know," she said, finally
looking at him.

"I do."

"You're called the executioner."

Remembering all the jobs he'd cut during the past couple
of years, he nodded wryly. "I can see that. It's not the only
thing I do, though."

When she didn't respond, he found himself impatient
for the way she had responded to him all those years ago.
Ridiculous but true. Her legs were still long enough to give
him hot fantasies, her hair sleek and strawberry-blond, and

her body held a few more curves than he remembered. He wondered how many men had passed through her life and felt a surprising stab of jealousy. "Are you married?" he asked.

She paused a half beat. "No."

"Will you join me for dinner?"

Her eyes widened in surprise. "No," she said with breathless speed.

He leaned toward her. "I need to explain. I need to apologize for never calling—"

She held up her hand. "I don't want explanations or excuses. I'm not interested."

Frustration coursed through him. He'd handled a dozen difficult situations better than he was handling this one. "But we had something special, and there's too much you don't know. You're acting as if this is the first time you've met me."

Her eyes flashed with anger, the first warmth he'd glimpsed since she'd walked into the room. "I can honestly say that this is the first time in my life that I've ever met Garrett Winslow."

He opened his mouth to disagree then remembered he had never told her his name. Ouch. "I should have told you my real name, but that trip was supposed to be my last escape from everything associated with my family name. I can't tell you how important it was for me to have you interested in me as a man, not a Winslow."

"I'm sure you had your reasons for deceiving me," she said, not mincing words.

He couldn't blame her for her anger. He would have felt the same way. It frustrated him that he didn't remember much about that last night he'd shared with her except making love to her over and over again.

"My father died that night."

She bit her lip and her expression softened a fraction. "I'm sorry. I'm sure it was difficult to lose him."

"In more ways than one. I remember making love with you that night, but—"

She sprang to her feet, her back ramrod straight. "I really don't want to talk about that."

"I don't remember anything after I got the call about my father."

She took a careful breath and dipped her head as if she'd traveled her own path of pain since then and had no intention of returning. "That's probably best."

"Why?" he asked, moving toward her. "Did you forget me so easily?"

"You have a lot of nerve asking me that. At least you knew my real name."

Frustrated at his inability to reach her, he shoved his hands into his pockets. "I missed you more than you could know. Please—I need the chance to explain."

Haley shook her head. "This is too much, too hard for me to take in. If you hadn't taken over E-Z, then we never would have seen each other again. I don't want to go back to what we had in Cozumel, even for a few minutes. I can't."

"Why? You're not married."

"No. But I'm committed. If you'll excuse me, I must go," she said, and left him smelling the faint sweetness of her perfume. He inhaled deeply. He had the gnawing sensation of wanting more.

If he listened to her, then he would leave her alone and let her go. She clearly had no interest in him. Seeing her again stirred up long-buried needs and wishes.

His chest ached with regret. He'd been forced to focus entirely on taking over Winslow when his father had died, and he had known he couldn't bring Haley into that kind of crisis situation. It wouldn't have been fair. By the time the worst of the crisis had passed he was a changed man, and he hadn't been sure she would want him. But now he couldn't avoid the gut-wrenching loss. Was there any way he could get her to listen to him? Should he even try? Garrett knew that nothing good came easy. He silently vowed not to give up.

After his last appointment, Garrett joined Bob Stevens for a drink in the hotel lounge. "You've done an amazing job," Garrett said, lifting his glass in a toast. "You built it from the ground up."

Bob shrugged and took a sip of his bourbon. "I just hope you won't cut too many of my employees. They're the reason the company has succeeded."

"I told you we'll try to let retirements and resignations take up any slack we might find. But you've run a tight ship. You shouldn't be worrying. You should be celebrating," Garrett said, patting Bob on the back. "You've just successfully negotiated the deal of your life."

Bob grinned. "I guess I have." He took another sip of his bourbon. "What did you learn during your employee interviews?"

"What you already know. They love you, and they're concerned about losing their jobs." He paused, seizing the opportunity to get more information about Haley. "Especially Haley Turner."

Bob nodded. "She's got a lot of responsibility on those slim shoulders."

"What do you mean?"

"I mean she's young. Single mother."

Garrett blinked. His gut clenched. "Mother?"

"Yeah, and she takes both jobs seriously, motherhood and her job at E-Z. The men call her no-man's land." He chuckled. "Mostly because she won't go out with any of them."

"So she doesn't have a significant man in her life?"

Bob cracked a grin. "It depends on whether or not you count a three-year-old son."

A son. Haley had given birth to a son while he'd been busy proving himself to all the doubters at Winslow Corporation. He couldn't help feeling another punch of loss. He also couldn't prevent his mind from doing the math. He had shared one amazing night with Haley four years ago. One amazing night where they'd been careful. The child couldn't be his. Could it?

Five

Haley's heart was still racing when she climbed into her car and fastened her seat belt. Turning on the ignition and backing out of her parking space, she struggled with a dozen emotions. He had recognized her and he still wanted to see her. Oh, heaven help her. Even though she was furious, looking at Garrett had brought back a longing she'd been certain was dead. Even though she had walked, practically run, from the office, part of her had wanted to stay and hear his explanation. It had taken so little to fan embers she'd thought were cold.

She couldn't help wondering how his life must have turned upside down when his father died. She wished she could have been there for him, comforted him. Life could have been so much easier if they'd had each other for the good times and the bad. She shook her head in disgust at herself as she pulled into the day-care parking lot. It still shouldn't have taken him four years to contact her.

She strode through the doors of the childcare center and caught sight of Jake. A surge of anger raced through her. For so long, she'd hoped and dreamed Garrett would come to her. She'd given up that foolish dream when Jake had taken his first steps. She couldn't allow herself to go back to that pain and uncertainty.

After driving home and closing the door of their small house behind her and Jake, Haley squeezed her son's little body. Her mind continued to race. Her instinct was to take Jake far, far away and hide. She'd worked so hard to build a good life for the two of them that she didn't want any disruptive intrusions. Plus, she knew that if Garrett ever saw Jake, he would want him. He wouldn't be able to resist the child that bore such a strong resemblance to him. And Haley didn't have the money to fight a custody battle.

Jake giggled and squirmed. "Mommy, that tickles."

Still trying not to panic, Haley took a deep breath and smiled. "Tickles? You think that tickles? What about this?" she asked, and lightly worked her fingers over his rib cage.

Jake laughed uncontrollably, and the sound of it soothed her fears. Haley had learned long ago that Jake's laughter had great medicinal qualities. In fact, she'd call it magic. She stopped tickling him and dropped a kiss on his forehead. "Do you want to walk Sparky before or after dinner?"

"Before," he said, his eyes lighting like firecrackers. "And after."

She laughed and ruffled his hair. "Okay, let me change my clothes."

The doorbell rang, and she automatically turned to open the door. Garrett stood on her front porch.

Her heart fell to her feet. She closed the door partway, but felt Jake wrapping his arms around her legs to crane his neck to see. "Who is it, Mommy? Who is it?"

"Someone from my office," she murmured, her panic returning full force. "Go to your room."

"But Mo-om," he protested.

"Go to your room," she said in a voice that brooked no defiance. She bit her lip at the hurt expression in his eyes, but she couldn't let Garrett see him. After Jake shuffled to his room, she stepped out onto the front porch.

Her heart hadn't stopped racing since she'd seen him in the courtyard. She'd dreamed of this for years, constructed wild fantasies and excuses for why he'd never called her. Amnesia or a kidnapping had been her two favorites. But after Jake had been born, she'd gradually snuffed out the embers of those dreams, and she didn't want Garrett stirring them again.

"I can't talk with you now. I'm busy," she said.

"We have to talk," he said, emanating a determination that made her want to run and hide. "There's too much that's been left unspoken for too long."

"That wasn't because of me."

"I know," he said, sighing. "It was because of me and my situation. I think we would both feel better if I had a chance to really explain."

Her stomach tightened and she shook her head. "I can't talk right now. I have other commitments."

"Your son," he said.

Haley's heart stopped. It took a full moment for her vocal cords to work. "How did you know?"

"Bob Stevens mentioned that you had a young son, that you're not married and you don't date," he added meaningfully as if he were referring to their previous conversation.

Haley swallowed over a lump of fear. "Then you understand why I can't—"

She broke off when she heard the sound of Jake's racing footsteps and the click of canine paws on the hardwood floor behind her just before the door swung open. "Mommy, Mommy, Sparky needs to tinkle!" Jake tugged at the hem of her dress.

Haley felt herself turn to ice. She saw Garrett drink in the sight of his son and knew in that moment that her life and Jake's would be forever changed. And not necessarily in a way that she would like. "Take him to the backyard, sweetie," she managed to say, then watched Jake drag Sparky to the rear of the house.

Her heart hammering in her head, she fidgeted with her hair. "As you can see, we're kind of busy, so—"

"He has your eyes," Garrett said, stepping toward her. "He has your green eyes."

She couldn't produce a word with him so close, so she nodded.

He tentatively lifted his fingers to a strand of her hair. "But not your hair."

"Right," she said in a voice she wished weren't so shaky. "He won't be called carrot top in school."

He gave a half grin, then his eyes turned serious. "Where's the father?"

Right here, she thought and fought a stab of hysteria. "He didn't want to hang around." She crossed her arms over her chest. "But we're fine without him."

Garrett nodded, his intense gaze belying his smooth tone and casual stance. "When was your son born?"

"He's almost three-and-a-half years old," she reluctantly admitted, knowing she couldn't hedge. She was desperate to end the conversation and the terrible awkwardness between them. "I really need to—"

"Is he mine?"

Haley's heart stopped. She'd wanted to avoid those three words more than anything. She forced herself to breathe. He stood there, so strong, so confident. What she wouldn't have given to have his shoulder to lean on during just a moment or two of the most lonely times in her life. But she'd been forced to handle it alone, and she and Jake had survived just fine.

"He is mine. I went through nine months of pregnancy, childbirth and weeks of colic by myself. Jake is mine."

"But someone is his father, Haley."

She shook her head. "No. I can't talk with you right now. You lied to me about who you were, had a one-night stand with me—"

"It wasn't a one-night stand," he said, his jaw tightening with anger.

"How many nights was it?" she asked sarcastically, hearing her voice crack at her remembered shame. "One. You promised me you would call me and you never did." She bit her lip, fighting tears. "My little boy wants to take the dog for a walk, and I don't want to have to explain why Mommy is upset, so you need to go."

Garrett's gaze held a world of pain and confusion. Some crazy part of her wanted to comfort him despite what she'd been through because of him.

Haley had to collect herself and have time to think. It had taken her a long time to stop wishing that Garrett would magically reappear in her life. Now that he had, she was shaken clear to her bones.

"I'll go," he said, and the lethal determination she read on his face frightened her. "But I'll be back."

Six

Garrett was more nervous than he'd been in years. He'd persuaded Haley—or more accurately speaking, twisted her arm—to meet with him at a local diner.

It took three phone calls for Haley to speak to him for more than thirty seconds. Garrett admitted that showing up at her house had been a mistake. He hadn't intended to upset Jake, but he'd been knocked sideways by seeing Haley again and learning he had fathered her child. He promised neutral territory, but he had to see her. They had to talk.

He'd suggested cocktails in the evening. She'd countered with coffee on Saturday morning. He couldn't remember a takeover that had involved more dicey negotiations. He couldn't remember a meeting that had been more important to him.

She breezed through the door of the diner dressed in jeans that faithfully followed her curves and a T-shirt that failed to hide the slight bounce of her breasts, with her hair pulled back in a low ponytail.

She may not have dressed to impress, but Garrett couldn't stop looking at her. He hadn't realized how much he'd missed her. She tossed a quick smile at the waitress, then searched the room. As her gaze met his, her smile fell, and he felt the pinch of loss. There had been a time when her face lit up whenever she saw him. He stood when she arrived at the table.

"Where's Jake?" he asked.

"Susan, a friend from the office, is watching him. She adores him." She smiled. "Everyone adores him."

"Including you," he said.

Her smile grew. "I'm the worst."

"Or in his case, the best," he countered.

She thought about that a moment. "Maybe."

The waitress took an order for coffee and left. Silence hung between them.

He cleared his throat. "An apology would be so inadequate that it would be ridiculous."

She looked down and laced her fingers together on the table. "An apology for what?"

"For not telling you my real name and for not calling you." He paused while the waitress delivered their coffee. "Growing up as a Winslow, I never knew if a woman wanted me for my family name. I didn't know if I could trust you. You were almost too good to be true. By the time I realized you offered me the real thing, it was too late. I stayed up all night last night trying to think of a way to make it right for you."

"And you can't," she said, lifting her gaze to his. "You can't change that you lied to me about who you were. And you can't change that you never called me."

He so wanted to capture her hands in his and hold her. "What did you do when you found out you were pregnant?"

"I panicked. I tried to find you, but you didn't exist. I had wild fantasies that you would reappear," she said, smiling sheepishly.

"How wild?"

"You had amnesia and had forgotten my name, but in my dream, you suddenly remembered and couldn't live without me."

He chuckled but felt a stab of sadness at how close she had come to the truth.

"I felt stupid and foolish. I knew better than to get involved with someone during a trip to Mexico. When I found out I was pregnant, I was so scared." She blinked her eyes at memories he wished he could take away. "I was afraid I would lose my scholarship," she said, shaking her head.

"You didn't, did you?"

She shook her head. "My grades suffered a little one semester, but I did okay." She took a sip of coffee. "It was hard realizing that the time you and I shared meant so much more to me than it had to you, but that's water under—"

"That's where you're wrong," Garrett said, unable to allow her to continue thinking that. "It may look that way because I didn't call, but I thought about you. I just didn't feel like I could drag you into my situation. When my father died, there was a fight for power in the company, and people were counting on me to come through. I was dragged through the mud and every day was a new crisis. By the time it was all over, I wanted to call you but figured too much time had passed." He shrugged. "I thought you'd moved on, and I wasn't the same man who walked the beach with you in Cozumel. I didn't know if you would feel the same way about me. But I never forgot about you. Never."

She bit her lip. "It looks like you did come through for the corporation," she said.

"But not for you. Or me. Or Jake."

"I don't mean to be unkind, but we've done okay without you."

"Maybe," he conceded. "But I'm realizing I haven't done so well without you."

Her eyes widened in surprise, and he felt a quick electrical awareness come and go between them. She bit her lip. "Our chance is over. Too much has happened."

His gut tightened. Something inside him wouldn't accept her words, but he knew now was not the time to fight her. "But what about Jake?"

She shot him a guarded glance. "What about him?"

"Are you going to deny that I'm his father?"

"I won't deny that you made a deposit, then left," she said crisply.

"Don't you think there will come a time when he will want to know his father? I'm sure you're a fabulous mother, but even you must know that he would need a father."

She sighed. "Jake is a great kid, and he deserves the very best. That's why I don't go out much. I want to find the very best man possible for him."

Garrett struggled with his pride. "What about his natural father?" he demanded.

She looked at him and shook her head helplessly. "I don't know how to say this nicely, but I'm not sure you're good father material. You may be loaded, great-looking and good in the sack, but you haven't always told the truth. You haven't kept some important promises, and you're a workaholic. I want somebody who is interested in Little League, soccer, telling bedtime stories and willing to trade cocktail

parties for Disney movies. You, on the other hand, are ob-
sessed with building the Winslow empire to new heights,
no matter what the personal cost is, and are known as the
executioner."

He felt the slow burn of challenge. "Are you telling me
I'm not qualified to be Jake's father?"

"Yes. That's what I'm telling you. A great sperm count
is not an indication of character or parenting potential."
Her cell phone rang, and she frowned, pulling it out of her
tiny purse. "Hi. What's up?" She listened for a moment,
her eyebrow puckering. "Oh, no. Okay. I'll be right there."
She looked at him and stood. "Sorry, I have to go."

"What is it?"

"Chicken pox."

He stood, not pausing a beat. "I'd like to help."

She cast him a look of doubt. "I appreciate the thought,
but this is really not your area."

"Maybe it needs to be if I'm gonna become father material," he said, meeting her gaze head-on. "I didn't have
nine months to get ready, but I'd like a chance to be the
man Jake needs as a father." And a chance to be the man
you'd have as a husband, he silently added.

Seven

Four days into his son's chicken pox, Garrett began to realize that watching the Disney channel hadn't adequately prepared him for parenting.

Although Jake was adorable, he was justifiably cranky, and Haley wasn't much better. She might not have the pox herself, but she was tired from being up half the night with Jake because she refused to allow Garrett to stay at her house.

Jake had initially been shy but curious with Garrett. But Haley had raised a loving, friendly boy, and Jake was becoming more outgoing every time Garrett visited. Jake was beginning to trust him.

It might be wishful thinking, but Garrett sensed Jake wanted a father figure in his life. He could tell Haley was nervous about how easily Jake had trusted Garrett, but he would prove she had nothing to fear.

Meanwhile, he and Haley had reached a truce of sorts.

He longed for the easiness they'd shared, but she seemed determined to keep him at a distance. And he couldn't blame her.

That didn't mean he was giving up. Each hour he spent in her presence reminded him of all the time he'd missed with her, and he didn't want to miss any more. He heard her laugh with Jake, and the sound alternately lifted his spirits and twisted his gut because he knew she didn't feel free to laugh that way with him.

Susan called and tried to persuade Haley to join her for dinner. Haley looked at her miserable son and gestured for Garrett to stop Jake from scratching. "I'd better not, Susan. Jake's at the super-itchy stage." She paused. "Yes, I know I have a babysitter, but he's not experienced and—" She broke off when her gaze tangled with Garrett's.

"I can do it," he said, walking toward her. "You're well-stocked with Benadryl and calamine lotion."

She looked at him doubtfully. "Yes, but…"

He saw a faint, grudging glimmer of trust and attraction in her eyes. "I hear you, Susan. I'm not being an over-protective mother." She frowned at the phone. "Okay, I'll come, but I'm not staying for more than two hours." She hung up the phone and looked at Garrett. "Are you sure you want to do this?"

"Never been more sure," he said, knowing this was his opportunity to prove himself to her.

"I'm not sure this is a good idea."

"It will help you to get out. You won't feel so…cooped up and cranky."

She gave a double take. "I haven't been cranky."

"Did I say cranky? I meant cooped up and tense."

"I haven't been cranky," she insisted, then left him biting his tongue.

When she returned from her bedroom, dressed in a skirt

that revealed her pretty legs and a top that clung to her skin, reminding him of intimacies they'd shared, she reviewed medication dosages and procedures. "Jake knows my cell phone number in case you forget," she said sweetly.

"Forget?" he echoed, his pride roaring to the surface. "I wouldn't forget your cell phone."

"Well, y'know, you did forget my other number a few years back."

"Very cute," he said. "But I didn't—254-555-6238."

Her eyes widened in surprise.

"I dialed it a hundred times in my brain," he told her.

A combination of vulnerability and something that almost looked like passion deepened her eyes for a moment. "I—uh, didn't know."

"There's a lot we haven't had the opportunity to learn about each other."

She nodded. He could see she was processing the new information. She cleared her throat. "Well, I guess I should go."

"We'll be fine. I know your cell."

"I guess you do," she said, her lips twitching. She walked to the door then turned around. "Have I really been cranky?"

"Do you want the diplomatic answer?"

"No."

"You've acted like a worried mother who wants her son to feel better and be well."

"I thought I said I didn't want the diplomatic answer." She chuckled, and the sound filled him with sunshine. "Never mind. I'll be back in two hours."

Within ten minutes, Jake began to itch and scratch. Evening was the worst time for the little guy, and no matter how often Garrett reminded him not to scratch, Jake couldn't seem to help it. He began to cry. The sound wrenched at Garrett's heart. He scooped up the child and put him in a lukewarm bath with baking soda.

The water provided some relief, but upon closer inspection, Garrett learned that Jake's mouth was filled with blisters. That was why he hadn't eaten earlier.

Garrett heard his cell phone ringing while Jake was in the bath, but ignored it. He knew it was his assistant calling about the negotiations he'd originally scheduled for this week but shelved at the last minute. It was a tricky situation, and he could lose the deal. His cell rang again, and he looked into his son's miserable gaze and let the damn thing ring. Jake's well-being was the only thing on his mind.

He took Jake out of the tub and tried to dress him, but the boy fussed. Garrett decided clothes were overrated anyway. He carried him into the den, set up a fan so that a constant breeze blew over Jake and pulled out a half-dozen books.

Haley arrived home to a house that was eerily quiet except for an odd beeping noise. For a moment, she feared something terrible had happened.

She rushed through the foyer to the den and stopped short at the sight of Jake sleeping, his head resting on Garrett's chest, while Garrett, too, slept. Her little boy was buck naked and generously coated with calamine lotion, but he was resting more comfortably than he had the past three nights. She saw a discarded stack of bedtime books and three Popsicle sticks.

"Popsicles for the blisters in his mouth," she murmured in surprise, wishing she had thought of it, wondering how the executioner could have thought of such a thing. Maybe because he wasn't really an executioner. Maybe because he wasn't the egotistical villain she'd tried to paint him in her mind.

Garrett still took her breath away. She thought she'd
buried her feelings for him, but being with him so much
reminded her how much she'd missed him. The way he
looked at her made her feel like someone had lit a fire-
cracker inside her. She had concealed her attraction to him
so far, but she wasn't certain how she could continue the
charade. His determination to know Jake chipped away at
her defenses. His gentle humor with her and the light in his
eyes made her heart stutter. Despite her best efforts, their
camaraderie was coming back; the magic between them
still simmered.

She looked at the two dark heads so close together and
felt her heart squeeze tight. She was looking at her secret
dream, a dream so secret she hadn't wanted to admit it even
to herself.

What if Garrett could be a good father to Jake? What if
she and Garrett could find what had brought them together
in the first place?

The forbidden questions terrified her. The annoying
beeping sound continued, and she walked toward it, finding Garrett's cell phone on the sofa. Business, she thought
and wondered if it was urgent. She wondered if he would
leave again. A knot formed in her throat at the thought.
More dangerous thoughts. She shouldn't rely on him. She
couldn't rely on him.

"Garrett," she said, awkwardly touching his shoulder.
"Garrett."

His eyes blinked, and he took a moment to focus. "Hi,
Haley."

Her heart thumped at the way he said her name. She
liked the way he rolled it around in his mouth as if he
wanted to savor it. Silly thought, she scolded herself. "Your
cell phone's beeping. I'll put Jake to bed."

"The fan's the key," he told her as she lifted Jake from his chest.

Jake stirred. "Hi, Mommy. Garrett gave me Popsicles to make my mouth feel better."

"I know. That was brilliant."

"They tasted good, too," Jake said, making her laugh. She put him to bed and returned to find Garrett on the sofa, raking his hand through his hair.

"Bad news?"

He nodded. "I'm going to lose this deal if I don't get back to Houston tomorrow."

Eight

Garrett was silent for a long moment, lost in thought. He didn't want to go to Houston at all. He didn't want to miss a minute with Haley and Jake. He chuckled to himself at the change in him. His job just didn't seem that important to him anymore compared to being with Haley and Jake. This was where he wanted and needed to be. He'd spent the past four years without Haley and he didn't want to go another moment without her.

"You should go," Haley said, wishing her chest didn't feel so tight and achy. "It sounds important. I can handle Jake."

"I'm not going," he said, flipping his cell phone shut.

She laced and unlaced her fingers. "But what if you lose the deal? This was a nice idea to try to be here during Jake's chicken pox, and you've done much better than I expected, but you're the big chief of Winslow Corporation.

Thousands of employees are counting on you to do your thing."

Nodding silently, he stood and walked toward her. He touched a strand of her hair and lowered his mouth, surprising the stuffing out of her when he kissed her. His lips were tender and searching. Her knees lost their starch, and she tried to stiffen them. Startled, she blinked when he pulled away.

"Nice try, Haley, but I'm sticking it out until the last scab falls."

"What happens after that?" The telltale question popped out of her mouth before she could stop it. She wasn't supposed to care what Garrett did, period.

He cocked his head to one side and gave her a slow, sexy smile that ruffled nerve endings she had thought were deader than a doornail. "I think it depends on what kind of evaluation you give me."

She frowned in confusion. "Evaluation? What do you mean?"

"I mean it's customary for the supervisor to evaluate the trainee after a special project."

Haley nearly laughed aloud at the implication that she could supervise Garrett the executioner in any area. "And the results of my evaluation will do what?" she asked, playing along.

"You'll tell me if I'm ready for a promotion," he said, sliding his gaze over her and heating her from head to toe. "I'm not staying just for Jake, Haley. I've missed you for four years. I don't want to miss you anymore." He lifted his thumb to touch her chin. "G'night. Call me if you need me."

Haley watched him walk out the door and struggled not to drop her jaw in astonishment.

She shook her head. It wasn't possible that Garrett would

give up the chance to take over another company to add to the Winslow empire. He wouldn't trade that to stay with Jake while he had chicken pox. It wasn't possible, she told herself. He would be gone in less than twenty-four hours. She darn well better not expect him to be hanging around her house when he could be pulling down a multibillion-dollar deal. The cold reality chilled her, but she forced herself to face it.

But the following morning, Garrett showed up at her door, and he did so every day until Jake no longer itched and his last scab fell off.

Haley fought her attraction to him during those days, but her heart wasn't nearly as sensible as it should be. Her heart should have learned not to count on Garrett. Her heart should have given up hope a long time ago, but somewhere buried deep inside, that darned little seed of hope pushed through the ground, as if it had been waiting for a spring thaw.

It was hard to stay cold when she heard Garrett make tugboat noises as he read a book to Jake. It was hard to remain untouched when she saw Jake make Garrett laugh. It was hard not to long for that special something she and Garrett had shared in Mexico.

After she tucked Jake into bed, Garrett waited for her outside the door. Her heart raced at the look on his face. She wondered if he was going to leave. The thought of it hurt so much it took her breath.

He laced her fingers in his, and she allowed it. She would have to consider why later. He led her to the sofa and took both her hands in his. "I want a promotion."

She bit her lip. "To what?"

"Anything above the slug who left you alone and pregnant would be an improvement," he said wryly. His gaze turned serious. "But I want more."

"You're Jake's father. I won't keep you from that. I can't. It wouldn't be fair to him."

He nodded. "That's important. I want that, but I want more," he told her. "I want you, Haley, like we were in Mexico."

She felt her eyes sting with the threat of tears. "We really can't go back."

"But you're still everything I've ever wanted in a woman. When I'm with you, I still feel that click inside me that tells me everything's okay. I want you. I want to know you as much as any human being can know another. I love you, and I want the chance to love the woman you're going to become."

Haley's heart felt as if it were going to burst. She swallowed over the hard lump of emotion in her throat. "What if you change your mind?"

"I won't. I never did. I just didn't think I could drag you into the mess my father left behind." He lifted his hand to her chin. "It's okay if you don't quite believe me. I just want the chance to prove it. If it takes a year, two, three or more, I'll be here until you see we really were meant to be."

"But what about your position at Winslow?"

"I've made arrangements to scale back on my workload. It's time for me to delegate more deals to my executive team while I take care of the important stuff. You, me and Jake. I can stand to lose a lot, but I never want to lose you again. And maybe when you're ready, we can revisit Cozumel. But this time, we'll come back together."

Haley's eyes filled with tears. "I don't know what to say."

"You don't have to say anything. Just let me prove my love to you. I love you, Haley."

"And I love you," she whispered, and it was the sweetest sound he'd ever heard.

Epilogue

There must have been something in the Cozumel water. They went to Mexico for their honeymoon, and Haley got pregnant again. But this time when she delivered their baby daughter with the wisp of strawberry-blond hair and Daddy's brown eyes, Garrett was with her the whole time.

While Haley caught a few winks of sleep, he kissed her on the forehead then took his daughter down the hall to meet her big brother. Garrett's heart was so full he wondered if it would burst. There was nothing more valuable than what he and Haley shared, and she'd just given him one more priceless little miracle of love.

* * * * *

PASSION

COMING NEXT MONTH
AVAILABLE APRIL 10, 2012

#2149 FEELING THE HEAT
The Westmorelands
Brenda Jackson
Dr. Micah Westmoreland knows Kalina Daniels
hasn't forgiven him. But he can't ignore the
heat that still burns between them....

#2150 ON THE VERGE OF I DO
Dynasties: The Kincaids
Heidi Betts

#2151 HONORABLE INTENTIONS
Billionaires and Babies
Catherine Mann

#2152 WHAT LIES BENEATH
Andrea Laurence

#2153 UNFINISHED BUSINESS
Cat Schield

#2154 A BREATHLESS BRIDE
The Pearl House
Fiona Brand

REQUEST YOUR FREE BOOKS!

2 FREE NOVELS PLUS 2 FREE GIFTS!

Harlequin® Desire

ALWAYS POWERFUL, PASSIONATE AND PROVOCATIVE

YES! Please send me 2 FREE Harlequin Desire® novels and my 2 FREE gifts (gifts are worth about $10). After receiving them, if I don't wish to receive any more books, I can return the shipping statement marked "cancel." If I don't cancel, I will receive 6 brand-new novels every month and be billed just $4.30 per book in the U.S. or $4.99 per book in Canada. That's a saving of at least 14% off the cover price! It's quite a bargain! Shipping and handling is just 50¢ per book in the U.S. and 75¢ per book in Canada.* I understand that accepting the 2 free books and gifts places me under no obligation to buy anything. I can always return a shipment and cancel at any time. Even if I never buy another book, the two free books and gifts are mine to keep forever.

225/326 HDN FEF3

Name _____ (PLEASE PRINT) _____

Address _____ Apt. #

City _____ State/Prov. _____ Zip/Postal Code

Signature (if under 18, a parent or guardian must sign)

Mail to the **Reader Service:**
IN U.S.A.: P.O. Box 1867, Buffalo, NY 14240-1867
IN CANADA: P.O. Box 609, Fort Erie, Ontario L2A 5X3

Not valid for current subscribers to Harlequin Desire books.

Want to try two free books from another line?
Call 1-800-873-8635 or visit www.ReaderService.com.

* Terms and prices subject to change without notice. Prices do not include applicable taxes. Sales tax applicable in N.Y. Canadian residents will be charged applicable taxes. Offer not valid in Quebec. This offer is limited to one order per household. All orders subject to credit approval. Credit or debit balances in a customer's account(s) may be offset by any other outstanding balance owed by or to the customer. Please allow 4 to 6 weeks for delivery. Offer available while quantities last.

Your Privacy—The Reader Service is committed to protecting your privacy. Our Privacy Policy is available online at www.ReaderService.com or upon request from the Reader Service.

We make a portion of our mailing list available to reputable third parties that offer products we believe may interest you. If you prefer that we not exchange your name with third parties, or if you wish to clarify or modify your communication preferences, please visit us at www.ReaderService.com/consumerschoice or write to us at Reader Service Preference Service, P.O. Box 9062, Buffalo, NY 14269. Include your complete name and address.

HDES11B

Harlequin® Blaze™
red-hot reads

Sizzling fairy tales
to make every fantasy come true!

Fan-favorite authors
Tori Carrington and Kate Hoffmann
bring readers

Blazing Bedtime Stories, Volume VI

MAID FOR HIM...

Successful businessman Kieran Morrison doesn't dare hope for
a big catch when he goes fishing. But when he wakes up one
night to find a beautiful woman seemingly unconscious on the
deck of his sailboat, he lands one bigger than he could ever
have imagined by way of mermaid Daphne Moore.
But is she real? Or just a fantasy?

OFF THE BEATEN PATH

Greta Adler and Alex Hansen have been friends for seven years.
So when Greta agrees to accompany Alex at a mountain retreat
owned by a client, she doesn't realize that Alex has a different
path he wants their relationshiop to take.
But will Greta follow his lead?

Available April 2012 wherever books are sold.

www.Harlequin.com

HB79679

*Taft Bowman knew he'd ruined any chance he'd had
for happiness with Laura Pendleton when he drove her
away years ago…and into the arms of another man,
thousands of miles away. Now she was back, a widow
with two small children…and despite himself, he was
starting to believe in second chances.*

*Harlequin Special® Edition® presents a new installment
in* USA TODAY *bestselling author
RaeAnne Thayne's miniseries,*
THE COWBOYS OF COLD CREEK.

*Enjoy a sneak peek of
A COLD CREEK REUNION*

Available April 2012 from Harlequin® Special Edition®

A younger woman stood there, and from this distance he
had only a strange impression, as though she was somehow standing on an island of calm amid the chaos of the
scene, the flashing lights of the emergency vehicles, shouts
between his crew members, the excited buzz of the crowd.

And then the woman turned and he just about tripped
over a snaking fire hose somebody shouldn't have left
there.

Laura.

He froze, and for the first time in fifteen years as a fire-
fighter, he forgot about the incident, his mission, just what
the hell he was doing here.

Laura.

Ten years. He hadn't seen her in all that time, since
the week before their wedding when she had given him
back his ring and left town. Not just town. She had left the
whole damn country, as if she couldn't run far enough to

get away from him.

Some part of him desperately wanted to think he had made some kind of mistake. It couldn't be her. That was just some other slender woman with a long sweep of honey-blond hair and big, blue, unforgettable eyes. But no. It was definitely Laura. Sweet and lovely.

Not his.

He was going to have to go over there and talk to her. He didn't want to. He wanted to stand there and pretend he hadn't seen her. But he was the fire chief. He couldn't hide out just because he had a painful history with the daughter of the property owner.

Sometimes he hated his job.

Will Taft and Laura be able to make the years recede…or is the gulf between them too broad to ever cross?

Find out in
A COLD CREEK REUNION
Available April 2012 from Harlequin® Special Edition®
wherever books are sold.

ROMANTIC SUSPENSE

Danger is hot on their heels!

Catch the thrill with author

LINDA CONRAD

Chance, Texas

Sam Chance, a U.S. marshal in the Witness Security
Service, is sworn to protect Grace Brown and her
one-year-old son after Grace testifies against an infamous
drug lord and he swears revenge. With Grace on the edge of
fleeing, Sam knows there is only one safe place he can take
her—home. But when the danger draws near, it's not just
Sam's life on the line but his heart, too.

Watch out for

Texas Baby Sanctuary

Available April 2012

Texas Manhunt

Available May 2012